Power
of The
Dark Realm

Power
of The
Dark Realm

Gardner McAdams

BOOK BOOK²

BOOK BOOK SQUARED
P.O. Box 60144
Colorado Springs, Colorado 80960

McAdams, Gardner
Power of the Dark Realm/Gardner McAdams
First edition, June 1, 2023

Library of Congress Control Number: 2023909021

ISBN 978-1-943829-47-7

Publisher's Cataloging-in-Publication data

Names: McAdams, Gardner, author.
Title: Power of the dark realm / Gardner McAdams.
Description: Colorado Springs, CO: BOOK BOOK SQUARED, 2023.
Identifiers: LCCN: 2023909021 | ISBN: 978-1-943829-47-7
Subjects: Interplanetary voyages--Fiction. | Outer space--Fiction. | Science fiction. | Romance fiction. | Love stories. | BISAC FICTION / Science Fiction / Action & Adventure | FICTION / Romance / Science Fiction
Classification: LCC PS3613 .C33 P69 2023 | DDC 813.6--dc23

Published in the United States of America by Book Book Squared
P.O. Box 60144
Colorado Springs, Colorado 80960

Book design and layout by Donald Kallaus and Susan Schorsch
Cover design: Jim Arthurs
Book Book Squared is an imprint of Rhyolite Press LLC

To my wife, Maria.
Inspired by our romance, I began writing
about the characters in this book within
a few weeks of meeting her.

Contents

You cannot use me up   You cannot destroy me   You
cannot change me

But use me   You have no choice in that matter   Do you?
It is in the ways that I am used that choice exists

I have no demands   And, you must only obey that which
you decree

You can hate me   You can love me
It makes not a particle of difference   You can even say that
I never came your way   That I don't exist

But I am here

Just use me   Use me to your salvation or as doom's pathway
I will provide the foothold

You may ask for validation   You may ask for justice
I leave all that in your hands   You may even say that I have treated you
unfairly

I also leave you to your beliefs   In the end,
Life's meaning lies in self-judgement

You ask   Do I love you?   I live through you

To enhance your reading pleasure,
a descriptive listing of characters,
places, and things can be found on
page 188.

Chapter 1

A Craft of a Different Sort

In their laboratory, Maritou and Gar, just to be sure, checked their instruments and then ran the experiment for a third time.

With Maritou sighting the gun, Gar asked, "Ready?"

"Ready. Charge."

Gar began recharging the concentrator with Invisible Matter. The deep thrumming of the force field generators reverberated up their tall and slender bodies. As the generators reached peak frequency, Maritou shivered from feeling the urge to open her wings and enjoy a good stretch.

Noticing her sensuous movements, Gar breathed deeply.

Maritou and Gar were Gentar, a species evolved from small, mammalian-like omnivores. By contrast, their Vulan shipmates were shorter and wingless, and alluring in their own right.

The Gentar and the Vula came from sister planets. Fifteen centuries earlier, in search of new homes, they made a pact to leave their solar system, together. The two races now shared this common objective inside an armada of asteroids they had fashioned into their spacecraft homes. Tethered together in groups and twirling around one another to simulate gravity, the asteroids provided superb protection from the dangers of space. Even the most powerful gamma rays could not penetrate the outer layers of their rocky world. The asteroids provided enough water, fuel, and raw materials to sustain them for thousands of years.

Maritou and Gar focused their attention to their instruments and, again, fired the cannon. A laser beam bounced off a nearby asteroid and returned to the lab's detectors. A graph on the computer screen confirmed the speed of the light.

Gar gasped, "We've broken the light-speed barrier!"

Maritou fluttered her wings. "I don't believe it. We've stretched space and controlled the direction of the expansion."

Gar added, "This is evidence of the true nature of Invisible Matter and Hidden Energy that has eluded science for centuries. It's like a battery. The Invisible Matter contains the energy source of the universe! And I think we will eventually prove that the atoms in regular matter are held together and powered by minute amounts of energy being drawn from the Invisible Matter."

Maritou shouted, "And without it, perhaps all regular matter would instantly unravel."

"I wouldn't want to be around for that," Gar replied.

"We still don't know the exact nature of space," Maritou said. "But we do know that when the energy in Invisible Matter is released it creates a pressure or, something else, that only influences space. And, I suspect that the expansion is absorbed by ambient space, much like gases are when the pressures vary from one region to another."

"Yes," Gar replied, "and our discovery is just beginning. We were able to release and control the Hidden Energy and this reacted with space and stretched it a bit. Now we can shift focus to find useful practical applications. I've been waiting until we had some concrete evidence to propose the next step in our research. Now that we have it, I can't wait a moment longer!"

"Yes?" Maritou asked.

"This may sound a bit crazy, but, in my imagination, I have an idea for the design of a super light-speed space craft."

At this, Maritou's body involuntarily recoiled.

Gar, whose eyes were no longer focused on his surroundings,

didn't notice her reaction. He was happily concentrating on his vision.

"Actually, my idea is not that original," he admitted. "It's a copy."

Maritou's throat tightened. "A copy of what, exactly?" She couldn't block out the sudden image of him inside a space ship speeding back to Planet Hogar—and back to Rena!

The reality of what he proposed put everything Maritou held dear at risk. *Gar loves me! I'm sure of that. But his love for Rena is even stronger!*

Soon after the Armada had headed off in search of new worlds, Gar's wife, Rena, had been carried off by his powerful foe, O'Ruhn. As O'Ruhn made his getaway, his ship was last sighted disappearing into the lower levels of Hogar's atmosphere. The rescuers' crafts were designed mostly for open space, and pursuit into the dense and forbidding depths, where O'Ruhn headed, would be impossible.

In the heat of his panic, Gar attempted to board one of the rescue ships, but the Vulan officers refused to let him go. He may not have returned. And, as one who possessed indispensable scientific knowledge, he was critical to the entire mission. Years later, well out of range for their ships to return to Hogar, the Vulans finally released Gar from imprisonment so that he could return to his duties as Co-Commander of the Armada.

After his imprisonment, Gar continued to struggle with his loss of Rena. The Mission's allies, back on their home planets, continued to look for Rena. But she had not been found. Gar had never received confirmation of either Rena's death or whether she still lived. And until the quantum two-way radio system had been invented, the radio communications between the Mission and the home planets had taken years on their one-way crossings.

Maritou needed to swallow. Her tongue felt like a dried-out sponge.

Gar went on. "There are significant obstacles but it's so beautifully simple really."

Maritou took a few sips of water and a long slow breath. As she released it with a sigh, the tension in her neck and shoulders eased slightly. Long ago, she had learned this technique to help with anxiety. *Ok, I can handle this! After all, immortals don't stay immortal if they crumble into heaps of goo!*

With a wistful smile, Gar announced, "Saucers!"

"Ok? What? Saucers?"

"Isn't it curious?", he continued, totally unaware of her discomfort. "We have had many sightings of alien objects briefly spotted, here and there, throughout our Mission."

"Yes?" Her voice sounded to her like it was coming from far away.

"Yes! Gar exclaimed. "Many of the witnesses talk of saucers, don't they? And, when I combine this shape with our new ability to manipulate space, I come up with ideas on how this might work. Using the saucer shape seems to offer a practical solution.

"Of course, perhaps the big challenge will be the fact that solid objects, like the crew and the ship itself, occupy space. There may be a limit to the amount of space warp that solid objects can tolerate. And if this is true, we must find a way to limit this effect within the confines of the vessel."

Maritou laughed ruefully. She had a sudden vision of Gar being twisted into a pretzel. "Otherwise, your teeth could end up a good many light years from your stomach!"

He reached for her and kissed her on the mouth. Her lips were a bit cold and he noticed her face was drawn.

"You look tired, my love," he said. "Let's just go up to the apartment and relax."

"Don't you want to spend the evening with Arohn? I know you are dying to share the news with him. And he does need to know."

Gar smiled and put his hands around her waist. His thoughts turned to the moments that they would share that evening. "That can wait," he said.

"Ok," she said, succumbing to his charms. As uncertain as her world might appear at the moment, she felt safe in his arms.

She pulled him close and, this time, their lips parted, igniting the passion they would later share.

"Do you think you can make us some bunuit?", she asked. "I'm ravenous!" At that, she bit his ear.

"I think you'd better save me for dessert!"

Arohn de Vul sat on a tall stool, his enormous head bent over the plans Gar was showing him. He was about half of Gar's stature, which was average for a Vulan. He and Gar co-commanded the Mission. Their friendship extended back, more than fifteen hundred years, to the Vulan invasion of Hogar.

Arohn had something important to tell Gar, but he waited, since his friend was so animated about this new idea.

Arohn pointed to the saucer in one of Gar's drawings rolled out on the desk.

"Are you sure this will work?"

"No!", Gar responded.

"But you believe in it, don't you?"

Gar flipped the page. "Let me show you something." The saucer lay on the page at a right angle.

"Huh? I was expecting it to fly flat like a children's toy zipping through the air."

"Yes, that would seem natural." Gar agreed. "But the Hidden Energy streams out from the curvatures at the top and bottom of the craft and expands space. Space expands more on the underside, and this provides a nudge, and the craft moves along effortlessly, like a raft in a flowing stream. Space seems to act similar to a gas, and the expansion mixes with the static space around it, seeking equilibrium. I am hoping that the shape of the craft will protect it from the considerable turbulence, preventing space from expanding too much, inside the ship. As the ship passes the turbulence, there is some additional expansion taking place on the underside of the disc, adding to the relative velocity."

"What kind of fuel drives it?"

"Invisible Matter and a small amount of helium, both of which are in abundance throughout the universe. The ship needs only to carry a small amount of conventional fuel, mostly for auxiliary needs and to start the generators. Once the helium ignites with the invisible matter, it produces all the power needed."

"I'm guessing it needs a lot of work." Arohn said. "What are the immediate obstacles?"

"Well, testing hasn't even begun. It's just Maritou and me. You are the only other one that knows anything about this."

"Where is Maritou, anyway? I would expect her to be here, too."

"She's not feeling well, today. I think she just needs some rest. She sends her love."

Arohn's face took on the same protective look it always did when a loved one had a problem. "Well, that doesn't sound like her. If she doesn't feel better, soon, have her come see me."

Fondly, Gar looked at his friend and smiled. "Ok, Doc."

"Anyway, I have some news," de Vul told him. "Le Noir called me and there have been some developments."

Arohn le Noir, "The Protector" was the Vulan Commander in Chief back in the home solar system. He was an exact copy of Arohn de Vul, made from his Original's DNA and a memory crystal. Copies are different than clones. Copies start life as if stepping out of their Originals at the moment of memory crystallization.*

Arohn swiveled on his stool and firmly gripped Gar by the shoulders. "There's word that Rena is alive!"

Gar's mouth opened and he allowed Arohn to steady him while he regained his orientation. "I knew it! Somehow, I just felt it all these years."

---

* On board the Command Ship were the DNA records and memory crystals of every Vulan and Gentar who elected to go along on the journey to new worlds. Duplicate sets were kept in secret locations back on, or near, the home planets. Room aboard the asteroid fleet was limited and, except for those born naturally during the mission, the living population was limited to essential personnel. The DNA and crystals in the Armada's storage, were used to reconstitute individuals, as circumstances and needs demanded. Someday, this dormant population would be reconstituted en masse to colonize new worlds.

Arohn and Gar held eye contact. Arohn's expression was a milder version of his protective look. "The information looks solid. O'Ruhn's son, Sten, made a visit to his father's stronghold. Sten spotted Rena and spoke with her. Despite being held prisoner for fifteen centuries, she appears to be in good health and unharmed."

Gar's hands opened and, when he realized that he couldn't close them around O'Ruhn's throat, he shook his head, in fury.

"What are the chances of rescue?" Gar implored.

"Maritou's Original is there with Le Noir and, together, they are working on a plan to rescue Rena."

"You know, with my Maritou's smarts, and her combat experience," Gar said, "she could help out with Rena's rescue plans."

"I agree! Ask her to come see me, right away."

Chapter 2

Emotion Storm

Maritou drew her bow. Wobbling slightly, she tried to ground herself in her archer's stance. Her combat instructor, Mendon Dahl, had taught her that the first rule of accurate archery was to eliminate unwanted tension, starting with the legs and wings. Today, her feet were telling her that something was terribly wrong. She had come to the range, after Gar left to meet with Arohn, hoping that she could immerse herself in a familiar activity and forget her fears. But her mind kept returning to the image of herself waving farewell to the man that had become an inseparable part of her existence.

Suddenly she had the image of Mendon, bidding her goodbye, so many centuries ago. Her chin fell to her chest and she let the tears flow freely.

This is strange! I've never before felt so much compassion for Mendon. Are these tears for Mendon, or really for myself? When I rejected him, Mendon must have felt then, much the same as I feel now.

Involuntarily, her body seemed to take control and, in less than a heartbeat she plucked an arrow from its quiver and sent it on its true path to the bullseye. She could find no such compassion for Gar at this moment. *I'm angry! It's as if he has already abandoned me!*

She stood there as in a trance for some time, unsteady on her legs. Unable to reclaim the solace that she had come there to find, she left and ambled aimlessly around the asteroid before returning to the empty and cold apartment.

She climbed into the unmade bed and into a dreamless sleep— sleep being her usual method of escape when life became unbearable.

With a kiss on the forehead, Gar woke Maritou. She pulled back slightly. He had no idea that she was beginning to surround her feelings with an invisible protective layer.

"How did your meeting go?" she asked flatly.

"Rena's alive!"

Maritou sprang to her feet. "Thank heavens! My beautiful friend!"

Maritou's Original, Maritou Venahus, and Rena had grown up together. For hundreds of years, they fought together in the wars with the Abaru. Maritou's love for Rena was unshakable. It was painful to see herself as Rena's rival, but that was the reality now.

For a long moment, her breathing stopped. She didn't notice until her body demanded a breath and she jerked at the sudden rush of air that quenched only the top of her lungs. Her shame filled her with self-loathing. *It was I who betrayed her! I'm a weakling!*

"O'Ruhn still holds her captive," Gar told her.

Maritou's eyes narrowed. "O'Ruhn must die!"

"Well, that may happen. Le Noir and Venahus are considering rescue plans."

Maritou stiffened, not allowing the sudden wave of self-pity to completely ruin the hope she now felt for Rena.

Gar's thoughts returned to the woman standing before him, and the recent changes in her that he could not ignore. He stifled the reflex to ask her if she felt better. He could see that she did not.

"Arohn asked about you," he said. "He asked if you would come see him. He believes that you can help with the rescue plans."

No reaction! Her mind was focused on some internal image.

He tried to embrace her. "Are you hungry?"

Slowly, she pulled back. "I'm afraid I am not very good company, right now. I think I will just go to the lab for a while. I have an idea that I want to explore. Then, I'll go see Arohn."

Something about her was different, and Gar wisely did not prod her. *It's one of those emotional chasms between the sexes. One where one or both sides could lose their footing if not careful!* It's not that their relationship would ever run out of passion. That wasn't the problem. It was intimacy that needed a kick start. And, so they ran from the truth, withholding essential pieces of themselves in fear that the other would not accept the full version of who they were.

Chapter 3

Expanded Space

Stepping into the laboratory, Maritou shivered. Not that it was much colder than their apartment. It was located just under the surface of the asteroid, just deep enough for protection from radiation but close enough to the surface to access a view of open space when the magnetic radiation field was activated, allowing the retraction of the heavy shields.

The cooler air usually felt exhilarating but, this time, she reached for the warmth of her lab coat before settling at her drawing board.

I'm so intrigued by this thing that threatens me so—this saucer! Why?

Her idea, if it worked, would require the formulation of a new material; not only strong and expandable, but one that could withstand the incredible forces of temperature and pressure emanating from its surface.

Immersed in the problem, the consequences of success left her mind, if only temporarily. For now, it was just her, and the idea that beckoned her forward. It consumed her thoughts, preventing them from turning toxic.

Let's see. If an object were immersed in an expanded space, the speed of light within that space would be magnified relative to its speed in regular space. That's simple enough. A bright school child would figure that out.

She knew, also, that taken to its immediate conclusion, the expansion of vast tunnels of space would require an unimaginable amount of energy—*totally impractical.*

But what is there to dictate the size of the expanded space? Perhaps it only needs to extend a minute distance from the surface of the moving object. And, as the object moves through space, it is constantly moving the expansion forward.

Gar's idea of the saucer shape is a stroke of genius! The curvatures of the dome and the underside allow for a differential in expansion levels which will allow the craft to exceed light speed in relation to the takeoff point. The object could actually be standing still in the space it occupies. It is the space that contains it that will be moving. The space beneath the saucer can be allowed to expand faster than the expansion above, effectively pushing it along.

Her thoughts turned to the objects and beings inside of the saucer, as well as the physical nature of the saucer itself.

Now, let's just hypothesize that solid objects keep their dimensions, no matter how expanded the space is that contains them. In other words, the space between objects changes but the size of each object stays the same. It is when an object is transitioning and half of it is in one intensity of space and the other half is in another, that it could be ripped apart if the transition is not gentle enough. Once the spacecraft and its contents have fully transitioned, this structural stress goes away. Exactly how much of this stress is tolerable is something that will have to be subjected to exhaustive testing. But so will everything else.

She began drawing some modified Gentar and Vulan pilots with large heads and long thin extremities. They seemed without beauty, having leathery hides, big eyes and very little definition to their faces.

She chuckled. *Well, if Gar shows up at Hogar looking like that, Rena will send him back! And who would want him then.*

Then, she realized that her drawings seemed oddly reminiscent of the drawings many witnesses had made who had purportedly seen aliens.—*Well, who knows?*

She sat back in her chair and, as her focus drifted from the inner workings of her analytical mind, she reoriented herself to her surroundings. Satisfied with her progress, she was feeling somewhat recharged.

She walked into the main lab area. Four private offices had been carved out around the perimeter when the asteroid had been refashioned for the mission. She, Gar, and Arohn each had one.

She looked across at the fourth office, the one meant for Rena. Its door, which she had never seen opened, beckoned her. Her fingers closed around the handle, but her arm froze—*Why do I feel like an intruder?*

This was the last place Rena had been seen before she was abducted. Gar had watched her enter. She turned to smile at him as he left for the Command Center.

It was from here that she was taken!

She withdrew her hand as if she had touched something hot. Suddenly, her vision of Gar rushing back to Hogar in a saucer, gripped her mind.

I'll go and see if I can find de Vul.

She didn't want to be alone with her raw feelings. Her kind and wise friend might be able to cheer her.

Maritou found de Vul in the Command Center and waited while he completed a call with Home Base via the Quantum Two-way.

He waved her into his office. "Come in! Come in!" he said and took her hands in a warm greeting.

"Gar has briefed you on what is happening back on the Planets?"

It had become customary for the travelers to refer to their native worlds as "The Planets" rather than "Back Home." This helped to sever the emotional ties to that which can never be again.

"All that he told me was that Rena is alive, and that a rescue is being planned."

"Yes, and I have just received an update from le Noir and your Original. It is known that O'Ruhn's flagship gets its main supplies from the Capitol on Mon Mari. Our forces are working on a plan to have a small rescue team stow away on one of the regular supply runs."

"I want to help. Is there anything I can do?"

"Perhaps you can! Remember when the Council sent forces to arrest BarOak?"

"Yes?"

"Well, after he escaped, his ship was searched and we found some blueprints of what we suspected to be plans for a giant vessel designed to operate in the lower atmosphere of Hogar."

"O'Ruhn's stronghold!"

"Yes, and I placed those plans in the Top-Secret archives, myself. They are right here in the Command Center!"

"And you want me to analyze them."

"Exactly. There is nobody more capable or trustworthy. If you accept the assignment, I'll have an office set up for you, next to mine. It might be a little like old times, when we developed the Quantum Radio, together." Arohn's voice echoed the fondness and mutual respect that they had come to share—Vulan and Gentar.

"Of course, I accept."

"I'll bring you the blueprints."

"Arohn?" she changed the subject. "I'm curious about something—Rena's memory crystals and DNA are here with us. Yet Gar has chosen not to have her restored to him."

Arohn hesitated before answering, knowing that the truth would be unpleasant. But he would not lie.

"I asked him about this once," Arohn said. "He told me that it would feel like a betrayal. And, that as long as there was a chance that Rena survived, he would not abandon her."

Maritou caught her breath and reached quickly for the comfort of Arohn's hands. She felt his elongated thumbs close gently over hers.

She resisted the urge to ask him if he thought Gar would go to Rena someday if he had the chance. Tears were beginning to form.

"I'm so scared! I don't want to lose him! I've never loved like this before."

"He loves you, too. I see it when you are together, and I hear it in his voice when he speaks of you. It's this saucer idea, isn't it?"

She fumbled for the answer. "I—I think my fear has been there from the beginning," she admitted, "and I chose to ignore it—willing to take the risk."

"I'm curious," Arohn nudged. "Is it possible that he will not abandon you, come what may?"

"Really?"

"Is it possible that you mean that much to him?" Arohn pressed gently.

She wasn't convinced. "It's possible, I suppose."

"Ok, just think about it—So, when can you start in on the blueprints?

Chapter 4

Reawakening

300 Years Earlier

The day started out like thousands of days before. Hundreds of thousands of days!

Gar rose and went for his exercises. This day, his regime included flying and weight training. Then he would bathe and eat before going to the Command Center.

Stuck in his grief, Gar, with diminishing capacity, lived his life in an endless ritual—alone! Long ago, he had closed his heart, pathetically pining away. Over time, even his feelings of loss had numbed. He felt nothing but fatigue and despair. Slowly, imperceptibly, he was starting to wilt, losing his immortality. His friend, Arohn, hoped that the discovery of the new planet home, that they hunted, would spur him into action, knowing that he would be needed to lead the transition of life on the asteroids to life on a planet. This might restore his sense of purpose.

As usual, Gar avoided the public spa at the end of his exercises, and headed for the private baths. He tried the door, only to find that the facility was being refurbished. He had no choice but to go to the crowded baths. Maybe he could find a small pool where he could bathe in relative privacy.

He stepped from the dressing room into the enormous bath

house that had been carved out of the asteroid, leaving the natural stone exposed. The earthy aroma of steam, infused with minerals of the two billion years old rock, was calming and brought back pleasant memories of his childhood when he had visited a high mountain vapor cave.

Having no use for art for the sake of art, Vulan craftsmen express their artistry in everything they make. The baths were a testament to the beauty and functionality of Vulan creations.

Caught up in his thoughts, his attention was drawn to three Gentar women in a pool he was passing. One had her head back, cradled in her hands intertwined behind the nape of her neck. Her nude body was arched back slightly, her eyes closed. She was beautiful, as were her two companions that were smiling at him.

The woman in the pool opened her eyes and was looking at him. He was not aware that he had stopped and that he was staring. Her breasts were filling with blood and swelling, pushing the tips forward into soft, rounded points. Involuntarily, almost imperceptibly, her legs opened. The unmistakable fragrance of her arousal reached him. He was helpless in the face of the unwanted feelings that now awakened his long dormant desires.

In her eyes, he recognized an emotional innocence. She wanted him—body and soul! He had seen that look before. She was falling in love with no rational thought of the consequences. Gar knew, that if he took advantage of her feelings, the sex would be incredible.

But he did not open the door for this. He knew he could not return the feelings of this irresistible creature, looking at him now, full of hope and expectation. He had broken many hearts in his youth but, this time, his compassion overcame his lust. Regretfully, he smiled at her as he walked away.

Time passed and, although he managed to avoid the public baths for a while, he was left with a newly awakened libido. One with a starving hunger! Unaware that this chance meeting had opened a new chapter in his life, he felt unprepared to navigate the return of the heartache from which he had been running for so long. He could not yet see the blessings hidden in the new waves of agony crashing over him.

Deep in his subconscious, healthy kernels of life, lying fallow for a millennium, began to stir. Now, watered with fresh and honest tears and bathed in the sunshine of hope, their tender shoots came into view for all to see.

Then, it seemed as if he was crossing paths with Maritou more often than usual. And he was seeing her in a different light. He was finding her more irresistible than the woman in the pool.

Am I setting myself up unconsciously, running into her on purpose? Maritou and Rena are best friends, more than friends, really. An unshakable sisterhood. This is just wrong! My word! Rena would never forgive us!

Entering the laboratory one day to work on some genetic research, he noticed that Maritou was in her office, and they exchanged pleasantries.

"What are you working on?" he asked.

"I'm trying to refine the Quantum Two-way. Right now, it works with digital and I am wondering if there is a way to switch to analog. It seems impossible. Would you like to see what I've come up with so far? Take a look."

He came behind her to look at her work. Leaning forward to get a closer look, his shoulder brushed the back of her head. She turned, smiling up at him. From there, it just happened. Before he realized it, he was kissing her lips. She stood and took him in a full-bodied embrace.

It felt so right, so natural! Their hungry kisses quickly turned into an open-mouthed feast.

"I have always loved you!" she confided.

"You're amazing! And I cannot help it. I love you, too!"

Inseparable from the beginning, they soon realized how much they needed each other in every way. They shared everything with each other it seemed, except their insecurities.

She did not tell him of the shame she felt at loving the husband of her best friend. Those feelings were there, despite the impossibility that the original Rena would be restored to him. And she denied the irrational fear that Rena would somehow appear and take him away.

And Gar? Whenever a wave of grief hit him unexpectedly, he chose to hide it, not realizing that it was part of a natural process, and that it did not necessarily threaten his love for Maritou. He did not know that grief is a necessary pain. It is the unnecessary pain of fear and shame that is possible to overcome.

So, like many others, they stuffed their negative thoughts and emotions and went forward not knowing that, one day, they would be put to a test.

Chapter 5

The Fire that Ignites

Present Time

From her meeting with Arohn, Maritou went to find Gar. Her fears would not prevent her from sharing her ideas about the saucer. Anyway, she was missing him and ashamed of pushing him away, earlier.

Finding the apartment empty, she went back to see if he was in the laboratory.

No sign of him, there, but a large drawing of his saucer lay rolled out on his desk. He had been working.

She put her hand on the seat of his chair—*Still warm.*

She sat and turned her attention to his elegant and artful illustration. The two Gentars, drawn inside the spacecraft, left the impression that they were excited—sexually aroused, in fact. She scrutinized the female. *Could that be Rena? Rena's hair is as black as coal, while that of this woman is ambiguous.*

Staring at the enlivened couple, she felt her desires for Gar stirring. The earlier instinct to withdraw from him gave way to a sudden longing.

She stood and quickly left the laboratory. *I hope I find him in the baths!*

Walking into the steam room, the delight of the earthy vapor crossed her palate as her eyes adjusted to the thick fog.

Maritou found Gar stretched out, face down, on a smooth slab of primordial rock, almost as old as the solar system where it had formed. She noticed that the stone was worn from centuries of use.

He jerked slightly to her touch but was instantly disarmed by the familiar caress. Opening his wings, his entire backside was exposed, inviting her to explore.

Her hand traced the outside of his thigh. Her arousal rekindled as she massaged his muscled body.

"I've been thinking about you," he murmured.

"Oh, yes! I can tell," she laughed.

"Let's go into one of the private baths," he suggested, even though they seemed to be alone at the moment. "I've been having a fantasy about you, and water."

In some of the private baths there were special tubs with carved perches lying below the water surface. They were shaped to allow a variety of positions for love making.

Positioning herself on the stone, she begged, "Give us a baby!"

Gentar women have complete control of their fertility and can choose to store sperm indefinitely or jettison it at any time. She had saved his seed from the first time she had captured it, centuries earlier. They planned to use this precious sperm, one day, when they both agreed the time was right. Her plea for impregnation, this time, was only meant to heighten their passions.

He took his time with her, taking and giving over and over, again. Over the years, their love making had continued to evolve, not always into new plateaus but sometimes into new ways of expression and new feelings.

He held her close as they finished.

"I don't know what I would ever do if I lost you." she confessed.

"Don't even imagine that."

His embrace tightened and he inhaled slowly, savoring the fragrance of her hair.

"Let's eat something light and then go to the lab," she suggested. "I have some ideas to tell you about regarding the saucer. We may not have another chance, for a while, because Arohn has asked me to help with Rena's rescue plans."

"I wondered if you had been to see him."

That evening, Maritou and Gar stood over his desk in the laboratory.

"Nice drawing!" Maritou laughed, squeezing Gar's butt cheek. "I saw it earlier, and decided I needed to find you in a hurry."

"I'm glad you did. I think I'll make drawing my favorite pastime."

She pinched a little harder. "Now let's get some work done."

Leading him into her office, she began to explain her ideas.

He carefully studied her drawings as she continued.

He gripped his forehead the moment he understood her theory—how the expansion did not need to extend more than a minute distance from the upper dome and lower surface.

"Genius!" he exclaimed. "This certainly merits extensive research. You know, the weightless lab on Asteroid B-112 would be a good place to test this. I have lots of equipment there. With your approval, I can run with your ideas while you and Arohn focus on the rescue plans.

"Of course! That is what I was hoping you would say."

Chapter 6

Joining Forces

One of Arohn's assistants, a Vulan woman, arrived at the Command Center to find that Maritou had taken over her office.

"Who are you?" she demanded.

"I'm Maritou le Rohn. We haven't met, have we?" Maritou responded in a friendly tone.

The assistant immediately changed her demeanor as she suddenly realized exactly who she was addressing. Caught off guard, she weakly responded, "I'm Lore Li de Mohn, Communications Officer."

"Good to meet you. You didn't know I would be here, did you?"

"No, I didn't," Lore Li admitted.

"Well, I'm sorry you had to find out this way. It must feel like an imposition," Maritou went on, her concern authentic.

Lore Li was completely disarmed by this charming Gentar. "No, it's okay. There is another office where I can do my work. I'll go there."

"If there are things in here that you need, please let me help carry them to the other office."

Lore Li graciously accepted Maritou's offer and, by the time they had made two trips, they had become friends.

Maritou settled into her new workplace and started making notes, including everything she could remember about O'Ruhn—his behavior, who he knew, and the events that led to the downward fall of his character and the rise of his power. O'Ruhn had been Maritou's lover for a while and she reasoned that few others knew him as well as Rena, Gar, and herself.

O'Ruhn and Gar had been best friends. That is, until the day they both met Rena. They fell for her in the same moment.

Arohn appeared with Lore Li in tow. "I'm told that the two of you have already met," he said.

"Yes, Lore Li came in this morning to find a squatter at her desk," Maritou scolded mildly.

If Vulans could blush, Arohn must have been doing it.

"Er, yes! Sorry Lore Li," he atoned. "I'm bad about that, I know."

"No harm done, Commander," Lore Li said, exonerating him with her lovely smile.

Maritou began to pick up on the unmistakable adoration in Lore Li's eyes whenever Arohn spoke. Except for a hint of a smile, he didn't seem to notice.

"What say you, if Lore Li acts as your assistant while you are here?" Arohn suggested. "She has the appropriate security clearance."

Maritou nodded to Lore Li. "I would like that."

Lore Li, returning the nod, handed her the blueprints that she carried in a heavy roll. "Me, too! Is there anything you need me to do straight away?"

Maritou unrolled the documents on her desk. "Let's see, after I look over these plans, we can start to copy them electronically and index them so that the three of us and the rescue team on Hogar will have access. For now, please take this list of persons connected with O'Ruhn and try to determine their current location and status. Any that are living and here on the Armada, we 'll consider interviewing. We'll investigate them all for their connections to our enemies, past and present. See what you can dig up. These are the people I remember as having any connection to O'Ruhn or his lieutenant, BarOak."

Maritou turned to Arohn. "You and Gar can undoubtedly add to the list. And would you run this by le Noir? I'm hoping that at least one of these persons has actually been on board O'Ruhn's stronghold or has information that could lead us to any current ties."

Arohn took Lore Li's hand that held the list and gently turned it in order to check the names.

Maritou followed Lore Li's reaction. *If he keeps ahold of her much longer, I think she will orgasm! How can he not know?*

"Please get me a copy," Arohn asked Lore Li. "I can add several names, especially in relation to BarOak."

BarOak was the Vulan traitor who had commanded the Vulan research vessel where the blueprints had been found after his escape. BarOak and Arohn were long-time rivals. His whereabouts were unknown but he was believed to still be with O'Ruhn.

"Good," Maritou said. "In the meantime, I will start familiarizing myself with these blueprints."

Arohn and Lore Li left Maritou to her work.

The blueprints depicted a monstrous craft with a labyrinth of corridors, pipes, ducts and cables. The multilevel vessel was football shaped and each of the master drawings represented the floorplan of each level. Each master was supported by pages of detailed designs.

The drawings were all stamped with the seal of the Vulan engineering firm, Vor Wex Design, and bore the initials of the draftsmen, engineers, the partners in charge and, in some cases, the unmistakable initials of BarOak and O'Ruhn.

These must be the original prints!

Later on, Lore Li appeared.

"I've found something interesting," Lore Li said.

"Yes?"

"Two of the Vulans on Arohn's list are thought to have been a part of O'Ruhn's inner circle. They both chose not to have their memories crystalized and they both stayed behind when we left Hogar. You probably knew that, but what really got my attention is that one of their wives, Dar Enock, chose to join the Alliance, breaking all contact with her husband."

"Where is she now?"

"She has come to be a trusted member of our crew. She studied and trained as a botanist and is currently in charge of the fungus production on the Acton Asteroid Group."

"Excellent work, Lore Li. Get all of the details you can find on her and we'll decide what to do next."

"By the way," Lore Li added, "I checked and the Acton Group is currently half a day away from us by shuttle—in case you decide to interview her."

"I can see why Arohn has given you such an important position on his team. I like the way you do things."

"Thank you, Maritou. Say, can I ask you something?"

"Of course."

"I hear many rumors . . . Arohn was married, right?"

"Yes. His wife, Lan Loa, was murdered shortly after our mission was launched. Her body was found in a private bath on our sister asteroid. She had been brutally raped and sodomized."

"That's horrid!" Lore Li shrieked.

"Yes, it was devastating. And, when efforts were made to restore her, it was discovered that her memory crystals had been stolen."

"The rumors are pretty accurate then and, I've been thinking."

"Yes?"

"The work we are doing . . . maybe we will uncover something leading us to her killers. If her memory crystals were not destroyed, they might be recovered."

"I've noticed that you seem to be very fond of Arohn," Maritou divulged.

"I love him!" Lore Li confessed. "And until the truth is known about the crystals—anyway, I want to help."

"Even if that means you may never have him?"

"I will not lie! I want him for myself. But, when I say that I love him, mostly what I want is for the grief to be lifted from his heart. He deserves that, one way or another."

Maritou was admiring her new friend, more and more.

Before she left for the day, Maritou stopped by the Communication Center and requested an appointment to speak directly with her

Original, Maritou Venahus, at the earliest opportunity.

She went directly from there to the laboratory, knowing it was the most likely place to find Gar.

Gar's drawings lay open across a large table in the central lab area but the lab appeared to be uninhabited. Gar's office was dark, and the door was closed. Turning to leave, her eyes stopped at the open door to Rena's office.

"Gar?" she called.

Silence.

"Gar?" she called, louder.

Still silence, but she sensed that someone was there, and she had the irrational thought that it was Rena, herself.

She approached slowly, sidestepping to get a wider view.

She whirled to the sound of a click behind her, her instincts taking over. Then, she noticed a pencil rolling toward her. It came to a stop on the floor at her feet. *The click must have been when it fell from the table.*

Turning back to Rena's office, a tall figure loomed in the doorway!

"Gar! Why didn't you answer me?"

"Did you call me? I think I fell asleep in the chair."

"Yes, I did call. I was surprised to see Rena's door open."

"Well, I go in there sometimes to think."

He embraced her, and her body surrendered to soft kisses under her ear. For the moment, at least, she was able to set aside her fears.

"How was your first day with Arohn?"

"Excellent! Lore Li is my new assistant. I'm sure you know her."

"Yes, I think she's a good choice."

"She's great. Say, when you have a chance, would you get us a list of anyone you think has had contact with O'Ruhn, especially after he turned on you. BarOak, too."

"I'll have it before you leave in the morning."

"Come over here," he said, guiding her to the drawings on the table. "This is one of the experiments I want to start with in the weightless lab."

"It looks pretty simple."

"I've designed it to determine two things, mainly. There will be multiple light sources generating beams of pure white light, aimed back at sensors. That will measure the light wave frequencies coming from various distances. Spectrum analysis should help determine the magnitude of expansion and how quickly that expansion is absorbed in the ambient space."

Flipping to the next drawing, he continued. "In this next experiment, objects of various materials will be suspended in the paths of the expanding waves. The effects on these objects will be observed to test your idea regarding the warping effect as expansion moves through solid objects. Then, if needed, this data may help us find ways of protecting occupants and equipment traveling through a space warp."

"I've put a lot of thought into those unknowns, myself," Maritou declared, "and I agree. Until some testing has been done, it's too early to get invested in any offshoots of the theory. Your approach makes perfect sense."

Maritou had something else to add, but decided to wait to see if Rena's rescue attempt was successful. It was obvious that the saucer project would soon need a math genius. *Who better than Rena, herself?*

With her thoughts returning to renewed contact between Gar and Rena, her fears came rushing back. Reeling back on her heels, Maritou imagined she was drowning, sinking face up in a dark and cold lake.

Gar caught her from falling backwards.

"Are you okay?"

In her vision, she sank deeper, below the surface, and she could see Rena and Gar, in the air above, laughing and flirting as they spoke with each other on the Quantum Two-way. One hundred and fifty light-years apart but with no distance between their emotions! Rena was explaining how she would engineer a way to send him her memories so that he could reproduce her.

"My love, what is happening?" Gar implored.

Gar held her head in his lap while Maritou slowly returned to the present and reverted to her breathing techniques.

The fear is still very much with me, she realized, *stronger than before.*

Gar put his hand to her forehead. She was in a cool sweat. "What is happening, my love?" he asked. "Let me take you to the infirmary."

"No, no. I just want to go home and get some sleep. Let's see how I feel in the morning."

Gar stayed next to her with his arm around her waist as they walked to the apartment.

As they entered their apartment, she said, "I'm feeling much better now. And I'm a little hungry."

Gar prepared a simple dinner and sat close to her while she ate. Then she went straight to bed and he lay next to her. She was asleep as soon as she laid her head down.

Chapter 7

Alter Ego

Maritou awoke to the ring of her portable. It was Lore Li.

"Your call with Venahus is scheduled for the fifth angle (the 'fifth angle' roughly corresponds to mid-morning). And I have some more answers for you when you get here," Lore Li told her.

Gar came into the bedroom. "Good morning," he said, kissing her forehead to check her condition. She felt normal.

"Good morning. I'm feeling much better," she told him as she prepared for her morning shower.

Gar knew better than to insist she go to the infirmary. Instead, he told her, "You do look a lot better, but I am going to send a medic to the Command Center to check you. It won't take much of your time."

"Ok," she agreed. "The doctor can probably check me out in less time than it would take to convince you that I'm fine. And I want you to stop worrying."

When Maritou arrived at the Command Center, there was time to talk with Lore Li before she took the call with Venahus.

Lore Li had compiled files on Dar Enock and many of the others on the growing list.

"Here is the list from Gar," Maritou said. "I noticed a few names on there that are not on my list. What have you found on Dar?"

"She has earned a spotless record from the time she joined the Alliance. Although her main assignment is growing the special fungus that sustains us Vulans as our staple diet, her passion lies in developing new varieties of fruits and herbs for Gentar consumption."

"Amazing!" Maritou declared as she read a list of Dar's creations. "A lot of these are favorites of my own."

"I'm guessing she will be cooperative if you decide to interview her," Lore Li suggested.

"I think so too," Maritou agreed. "Let's send for her straight away. Would you clear this with Arohn?"

"Sure."

"It's time to speak with Venahus. I'll get back to you. It's good to have you on my team, Lore Li,"

Although the two Maritous had not spoken to each other for a while, they wasted no time. When an Original and their Copy talk to each other, there's rarely the need for small talk.

"We have some new developments." Venahus informed her Copy. "Le Noir is off to rescue Rayloh and Naomi."

Rayloh Cari and Naomi Kamara were not copies. They were clones of Gar and Rena; born and raised by surrogates.

"What happened? I thought Rayloh was successful in securing the contract to go forward with Operation Freedom." *

---

* Operation Freedom was Rayloh's plan to save Hogar from a colossal planetary collision with the dwarf planet Vespi; the next planet out from Hogar. It was the iron core remains of an earlier collision with Eo Phi. In the same planetary orbit, it had come up from behind Eo Phi. The massive collision left debris orbiting around Eo Phi which eventually coalesced into Eo Phi's magnificent moon. Vespi lost enough velocity in the encounter, that It settled into a degrading orbit around the sun and into a slow death dance with Hogar.

Rayloh's plan was to use Krell, a giant asteroid, as a gravitational tractor to pull Vespi into a safe and stable orbit. But O'Ruhn and his cronies in industry and the military had their own ideas. Rayloh and Operation Freedom needed to be eliminated.

* * *

"He was. Unfortunately, O'Ruhn cannot tolerate losing control and has decided to assassinate Rayloh and have him out of the way permanently. Le Noir found out because he listens in on the communications between O'Ruhn and his henchmen. He's had them bugged for a long time. Since Naomi might become collateral damage, le Noir will attempt to rescue her, too."

"How will this affect the plans to liberate Rena?"

"Le Noir left so quickly, there was little time for discussion. The supply runs to O'Ruhn's flagship are scheduled at fifteen-day intervals. We will probably delay until the following shipment.

"Has a rescue team been selected?" Maritou ask her Original.

"Because of the infiltration method, the team is limited to three. O'Ruhn's son, Sten has volunteered to go."

"That seems unusual, but I'm sure you know the risks."

"Sten knows the vessel and, more importantly, has a confidant on board; a crew member who can establish communication with Rena as the rescue unfolds."

"That leaves two positions open for seasoned veterans. I'm thinking that you will be one of them."

"That is the plan, so far. I do have the most combat experience. Le Noir is a for sure. Catching them off-guard is essential, and that is another reason to include Sten."

"I will be sending you a copy of the blueprints later, today. I'm sure that they will help you to plan the assault. I'm working on identifying the weakest parts of their defenses and will keep you informed."

"Good," Venehus said. "If we can identify the Command Center and the places where we can most likely find O'Ruhn, it will help us infiltrate the ship without detection."

"Well, I've identified the cockpit, which is connected to a larger set of rooms that probably comprise the Command Center. And there is another area, close by, which probably contains the security operations. If so, that is where the main battery of video monitors will be."

"Wow! You have been busy."

"And we should know more, soon. We have identified an individual, here on the Armada, who may have been on O'Ruhn's ship. We plan to interview her tomorrow."

"When we have the plans, here, I'll take them to Sten. He knows the ship pretty well, at least most of it."

They signed off with as little to-do as when they said hello, using the nicknames they had chosen for themselves.

"Good-bye, Venahus."

"Good-bye Number II."

Chapter 8

Lightning Bolts

When Maritou and Lore Li came into the conference room, Dar was seated at a small round table in the middle of the room.

Maritou noticed Dar's excellent posture, clear eyes and flawless skin. *Here is a person with a purpose in life.*

"We apologize," Lore Li began. "Your presence here has nothing to do with the ostensible reason that was given in our summons. That was necessary for security purposes. Let me assure you that you are not in any kind of trouble nor under suspicion for anything. However, everything we will discuss here is classified as Secret at the highest level."

"Okay," Dar responded, and rubbed the back of her neck. "I'm wondering if this has something to do with my marriage to Brim Lao. Has he done something?"

"That's very perceptive of you, Dar. But first, my name is Lore Li and this is Maritou le Rohn."

"Hello! Thank you for coming. Please, just call me Maritou. Can I call you Dar?"

"Yes, please!"

"First of all, please forgive me for the many questions we must ask," Maritou said. "It's just that we are under a time constraint."

"That's fine. Go ahead."

"Well, first of all, we are curious whether you ever had direct contact with O'Ruhn or BarOak, and if you may have set foot on O'Ruhn's flagship."

Dar did not hesitate. "Yes, my husband, Brim Lao and BarOak were closely aligned, and I knew BarOak before the Vulan invasion of Hogar. And later on, I had several contacts with O'Ruhn, mainly during social events on his vessel. But the first time I saw him was on one of the large Abaru islands. That is where I learned that he was trafficking in the Abaru."

"Please continue," Maritou urged. "What can you tell us about his flagship?"

"My husband took me there for its maiden voyage, which was an event lasting several days. It was so long ago and it's hard to remember the details. But I do remember that was the time we had a tour of practically the entire ship."

Maritou went to a desk at the side of the room and returned with a tablet. She drew a large oval. "Let's say that this is the main deck where the Control Center is located." She penciled in the floorplan at the nose of the ship. "Did the tour include the cockpit and the Control Center, here?"

"Why yes! Your drawing is helping me remember." Dar pointed to an area behind the Control Center. "And these are the resting quarters for the pilots and officers. The guest rooms, where we always stayed, are back here at the tail but on the next level up. Somewhere, here, in the middle, on the main level, is a grand ballroom, the main dining area, and kitchens."

"You have a great memory. Did you get a tour of O'Ruhn's quarters?" Maritou asked.

Dar's breathing stopped and, after a notable pause, she responded in a faltering voice. "No, I didn't, but BarOak's wife did. This was years after the maiden voyage, during one of the Inner Council meetings."

Dar's eyes watered and lost focus. "I . . . I'm sorry! After all these centuries, it's hard to believe that these feelings are still there—trapped inside my body."

Lore Li went to her and touched her, both hands gently massaging her shoulders.

"That was the day I decided to leave my husband," Dar declared, releasing the words never before spoken. "The wives were gathered that day, in the dining hall. BarOak's wife started boasting about her experiences the night before in O'Ruhn's private rooms. She described it as a sex party. But it was more than that—much more," Dar said, choking on the words.

"Just take your time," Lore Li encouraged gently.

"Well, by that point in time, we Vulans had a reliable supply of the 'Life Blood' fungus and it was no longer necessary for us to survive on Gentar flesh."

A long silence followed. Finally, Dar burst out, "But O'Ruhn had them doing it for pleasure! Even the Gentar members were raping and cannibalizing. O'Ruhn had supplied them with young Gentar from the Abaru tribes."

"And your husband took part in all this. And that is why you left him," Maritou ventured, filling in the next part for Dar.

"Yes!" Dar answered, relieved not to have to continue.

Dar closed her eyes. Maritou and Lore Li remained silent as Dar composed herself.

Finally, Dar said, "One other thing you might want to know—"
"Yes?"

"Ben Ru—" Dar spoke the name of one of the Gentar captains and the head of the space observatories on the Centex asteroid group.

"Captain Ben Ru?" Maritou asked.

"Yes, he was there that night."

Maritou sat back in her chair, taken by surprise. She wondered how Ben Ru's connection to O'Ruhn could have been overlooked when he was chosen for his position.

"I didn't know until recently, that he was here with us on the Armada," Dar explained. "I had only seen him, that one time, when we were on Hogar. He had a different name, then, but I haven't been able to remember it. Ben Ru wasn't a member of the Inner Council.

"No?"

"No. The rumor was that he was a slave trader. That night, at dinner, he sat between O'Ruhn and BarOak. It was clear that the three of them shared a special sort of brotherhood."

"Somehow, you found out that he's here on the Armada." Maritou coaxed.

"He came to see me. He acted very friendly. He told me it was good to be away from the murky depths of Hogar and to now be a part of, "The Great Adventure," as he called it."

Dar threw her hands up as if catching something that had been tossed to her.

"I wanted to believe him. I didn't know what to make of it."

Her hands remained in front of her face, as if she were holding a large ball.

"It was the friendliness. He was too friendly."

Dar's hands shot forward, throwing back the imaginary ball. "I suspect that he had other motives."

Her eyes connected with Maritou's.

"I did wrong, didn't I, keeping it to myself?"

"You must have had your reasons," Maritou said.

"Well, I somehow felt as if it were I who was being exposed. I love my work and felt threatened. When nothing happened after that, I thought it best to just keep it to myself."

"Look," Maritou assured her, "you are not in trouble with us. But for your security, you should not return to the Acton Group until we have investigated Ben Ru and we can ensure your safety."

From their meeting with Dar, Maritou and Lore Li went straight to confer with Arohn and gave him a full briefing.

"Let's get our security team on this," Arohn said.

"Yes, this is getting far beyond the limits of my spying capabilities," Maritou admitted. "But I would like to work closely with them if I can."

"Of course! They will answer directly to you."

Arohn turned to Lore Li. "Please go send word to Colonel BeCholn to come here immediately."

Arohn wanted a word with Maritou, in private. "It's obvious that we are suspecting the same thing," he began. "This Captain Ben Ru may have had a role in the abduction of Rena and...," his voice turning low and hoarse, "other things."

He was referring to the rape and murder of his own wife, Lan Loa.

Maritou returned his candor. "When he is questioned, let's get his DNA. If he was the one who stole Rena's DNA records, he may have altered his own records at the same time. If his real DNA matches the evidence from the crime scene, well..."

She gave him a reassuring embrace.

"I can use any advice you can give me in this investigation," she said.

"I suggest you and BeCholn coordinate closely with le Noir. You might not know this, but my Copy has become quite the security expert himself. He and his team have, for centuries, been searching out the identity of a mystery man, Code Name: "Bakus". Perhaps you have found him."

"Good! Le Noir will probably do this anyway, but we'll ask him to investigate those who vouched for Ben Ru."

Arohn's secretary rang, announcing the arrival of BeCholn, who then walked into the office.

Handsome and very tall, BeCholn had the same expressionless look on his face that Maritou remembered from the 1500 years she had known him. He nodded to Maritou and turned silently to Arohn, waiting for orders.

"Maritou has uncovered something big, Cole."

Cole was the nickname Arohn had bestowed on BeCholn, perhaps to make him seem more personable.

"She may have found Bakus."

Cole turned his eyes to Maritou. Did she detect a slight lifting of his eyebrows? She wasn't sure, but she definitely noticed the dilation of his pupils.

"If it's Bakus he's been here with us on the Mission, as we've always suspected?" Cole declared in a part statement, part question.

"Maybe." Maritou noted. "We suspect It's Captain Ben Ru and, if so, I'm sure there are plenty of accomplices with him."

"Maritou will take the lead on this," Arohn told Cole. "Help her in any way you can. I will brief le Noir and you and Maritou can coordinate with his team. You might start by investigating anyone who may have aided Ben Ru in obtaining clearance for the Mission."

Maritou and Cole withdrew to his offices to formulate their first steps.

Chapter 9

On the Same Page

Gar heard a fan come on in the weightless lab. He noticed that it took a few moments before he felt the wind blast.

Hmm! If space behaves like a gas, seeking an equilibrium with surrounding space, and an expansion of space acts similarly to the wind from a fan—Yes! This supports Maritou's theory. All that is needed to propel the saucer through the expansion, in front of the craft, would be a more powerful expansion behind it.

It follows then, that to move an object, in this way, would not necessarily require massive amounts of energy, because the magnitude of the respective expansions at the front and rear of the object would continue to increase the longer the energy source, causing the expansions, was turned on. Again, this is because of the delayed effect. The equalizing of space is far from instantaneous and space expansion would build up, in front of, and behind the space ship.

Okay? Now how can I test this?

It was late when Maritou and Cole finished and she had returned to her own office. There was a voice message from Gar waiting for her:

If you have any energy left when you finish up today, meet me at the weightless lab. I think I have found something interesting. I've ordered some food and maybe we can just spend the night here.

She picked up the phone and spoke with the Communications Center, requesting a secure line.

"Hello, my love. I got your message."

"How are things going there?" he asked.

"Good, good. But some things have come up and I will be working very late—maybe all night."

"Sure! What I have can certainly wait. And we knew when you started, that you might get into a time crunch," he told her.

"I knew you would understand. See you, soon. I adore you!"

"Me too! And I am so proud of you! See you tomorrow night."

She felt a warm glow as she turned her attention to her work. She shuffled through the blueprints, making notations based on what she had learned from Dar. The prints were already copied to electronic form, but Maritou preferred to work with paper and then transfer it to the computer files. It gave her a better sense of connection.

Dar had confirmed Maritou's hunch that O'Ruhn's private quarters and party chambers lay in the nose of the ship, on the level below the Command Center. The plans showed what must have been a small barracks behind O'Ruhn's suites. That was undoubtedly where O'Ruhn's bodyguards were stationed. The only corridor of any size that led in and out of O'Ruhn's quarters extended to the other side of the barracks to a secured entry.

There were only two other ways to get in or out of the chambers; one of these was only wide enough for one person. *This could be an emergency escape route for O'Ruhn. The other route was a long corridor that led back to what looked like a group of holding cells. From there, there was no direct route to and from the Command Center. This leaves the chambers vulnerable should the bodyguards be overpowered.*

Looking at the holding cells, if that was what they were, she shivered to imagine young Abaru slaves making their last stop-off there, unaware that they were about to walk into a chamber of horrors. *This is the least defended route.*

She sent a message for the other Maritou to radio back as soon as possible, and she received an immediate callback.

"Number II?"

"Good morning."

"Yes, good morning," greeted Maritou Venahus from Hogar. "Le Noir is back. Rayloh and Naomi are safe, here with us."

"That's wonderful! How are they?" Number II asked.

"They're recovering from the shock. They had never seen a Vulan before and when they witnessed le Noir eliminating their assassins, they feared that they would be next. They are a bit traumatized."

"And they've had no idea that they are clones, have they?"

"None whatever. We will be busy, for a while, helping them adjust to their new lives. Right now, they are both angry to have been taken from their home and cut off from the activities they were immersed in."

"Anyway," Venahus continued, "we should talk about Rena's rescue. You must be calling because you have made some progress. We have received the blueprint files, and I'm looking at them now."

"You'll be receiving a new set that is captioned and labeled based upon what we have learned from Dar Enock, the person I told you about. She has been on O'Ruhn's flagship several times."

The two Maritous discussed various rescue plans as Venahus made notations on her copy of the blueprints based on what Number II had learned from Dar.

At the end of the call, Number II sat back in her chair. Instead of feeling exhausted from being awake for almost two days, she was charged.

She thought of Gar. *He's probably snug in his sleeping bag. If I'm really quiet, I could sneak in and unzip him before he awakes.*

She pictured herself there, her hand softly caressing his abdomen. A wonderful and erotic fantasy played out in her mind. In her imagination, he didn't wake immediately but, instead, he started to incorporate her caress into a dream.

She didn't even care if he dreamt of another, or even more than one lover. In fact, that wouldn't be so bad. She knew from her own dreams that this was natural. If she could just bring him to a phantasmagoric plateau, and keep him there, on the edge—Oh! What a delightful memory that would make for both of them. It would supercharge their love making for some time to come.

"I'll be at the weightless lab, if anyone needs me," she told the officer on duty. "But only if it is urgent."

Chapter 10

Carving Lessons

The pilots were off-duty when Maritou arrived at the shuttle port, so she commandeered one of the smaller crafts and headed straight for Gar.

Impatiently she stomped her foot when she arrived, waiting as the docking chamber pressurized.

As she waited, she noticed that the self-pity she had experienced over the last few days, had evaporated. The progress that she and Lore Li were making was restoring her empowerment.

Finally, she winged her way through the entry shaft when the inner hatch opened. The main chamber of the laboratory was quite large. She used it regularly to train in weightless conditions, so she was familiar with the workings of the lab and the asteroid that contained it.

The lights in the lab had been turned down low and she didn't see Gar, at first. Then, her eyes were drawn to something gently floating in the semi-darkness at the far side of the chamber.

There he is.

Apparently, he had fallen asleep, working, and was slumbering in the comfort of zero gravity.

As she approached, his body posture struck her as comical and she muffled a laugh. Nearer still, she focused on the dark shadow she saw on the side of his face.

What! It's blood!

Sensing movement behind her, she whirled. The flash of a blade streaked by her neck. Reflexes and centuries of training and combat took over. Spontaneously, her foot shot out and connected with the wrist of the hand holding the knife. But the assailant managed to hold on to his weapon. Her move had pushed her and her attacker apart and she knew her flying speed would give her the advantage.

But suddenly, there was a strong hand gripping her forearm and another, her bicep, just above the elbow.

"You're dead!" Came the triumphant words of her second assailant as he held her for the slashing attack that seemed imminent.

Maritou's wings moved in unison, and a surprised attacker found himself, and his victim, rolling one way and then another into the trajectory of the blade. He screamed in anguish, his arm cut to the bone.

Letting go of Maritou, he was too stunned to stop his spinning. He resembled a slow-motion firework, his blood streaming out in a spiral as he twirled.

The remaining assassin unsheathed a second knife, much larger, almost a sword. Her best advantages now were her speed and, hopefully, her wits.

She drew her attacker away from Gar and spotted a fan that was set up to cool the test equipment. She ripped it from its anchor and wielded it as a shield. But it was only a decoy to trick her foe, who did not expect her next move.

His line of sight partially blocked by the fan, she was suddenly behind him, expertly snapping a wing tip. Try as he might, after that, she was able to outmaneuver him. He screamed in pain and defeat as she dislocated his other wing.

"Let the knives go before I rip off your balls!"

His hands went up and released his weapons. He knew she wasn't bluffing.

She pushed him with her foot to the far side of the lab, where he would remain until she could summon help.

Gar's body had drifted a bit toward the center of the lab. When she reached him, she saw that his face was now completely covered with blood.

"Gar! Gar!"

She quickly wiped blood from his neck, trying to find the wound! She checked his breathing and pulse. He was alive! She found a nasty bump on his head, just above the ear, that was oozing blood, but no other source of bleeding.

From her left came a whimpering cry. She turned to look, and a scarlet stream pulsed out from the arm of the twirling attacker. She found a cord holding one of the sensors for Gar's experiment and used it as a tourniquet on the assailant's arm to stop the bleeding. *The blood on Gar's face is not his own!*

Gar moaned and started to move. He tried to stand up, forgetting that he was in zero gravity.

"Where—"

"I'm here, my love!" Maritou told him. "You're still in the weightless lab and you've been hit on the head. You are going to be fine. Don't try to get up."

She pulled out her portable. "Cole? I'm here in the weightless lab with Gar. Bring medics, we've been attacked . . . No, I was able to neutralize them . . . Two attackers. They're both alive. One of them needs blood right away . . . Okay, call when you arrive."

She turned back to Gar. "Are you okay, my darling?"

He was feeling the knot on his skull. "I . . . I think so."

"I'm going to leave you here, for a moment. There are a couple of things I need to do here in the lab before help arrives. Call out if you need me." She kissed the cleanest part of his head that she could find.

Then, she secured the hatches in case there were more assailants and went to the weapons cabinet. She strapped on a pistol and grabbed the medical kit and a sleeping pouch.

She must keep the bleeding assassin alive, if she could. He had lost a large amount of blood, already. The only thing she could do now, was to check the tourniquet and keep him warm inside the bag.

He was unconscious when she got to him. His breathing was shallow and his pulse faint but the bleeding was in check. She slipped him into the pouch.

She looked at his comrade. He was studying her. Was that admiration she detected?

"Who are you, and why have you attacked us?"

"Who attacked who?" He countered ruefully.

Her portable rang. Cole had arrived.

Chapter 11

Shades of Betrayal

Arohn phoned Cole as soon as Maritou arrived in his office the next morning. "She's here, Cole. Are you ready for us? . . Okay, we'll come straight away!"

"You look fit, this morning," he told Maritou. "And how is Gar?"

"He's sleeping. He'll be fine! But you probably got a report from his doctors before I did."

He chuckled because it was true, and he picked up the phone, again.

"Lore Li? . . . Yes, we're ready. Meet us in the hall."

The three of them walked the short distance to Cole's office where they were ushered into the nerve center of Security Headquarters.

Cole and another agent were at one end of a conference table discussing the documents displayed on wall monitors. The wall to the right was glassed off from a larger room where several security personnel with head phones were glued to their surveillance monitors.

Cole gestured to the new arrivals. "Please, come sit where you can see the screens."

He used a remote to bring up the image of a distinguished looking Gentar. Maritou recognized him as the bleeding attacker.

Another monitor showed a live feed from his hospital room.

"This is Ben Ru," Cole said flatly, referring to the file photo on the left monitor. "And that's him recovering from a massive loss of blood. He's slowly regaining consciousness. We'll interrogate him when he wakes up."

Cole pointed his remote and an image of the knife wielding attacker appeared.

"This photo of the other assassin is one taken recently for his access card renewal." Cole clicked again. "Now, this photo is much more recent," Cole said in a slightly ironic tone and he looked around for reactions.

Maritou's eyes flashed a moment of surprise and silent laughter at Cole's stab at humor. It was a photo of the broken wing tip.

Cole, encouraged by Maritou's approval, kept joking. "His name is Sauhn Lin but I'm thinking of changing it to "Sawn Limb.""

This brought laughter all around and brightened the mood.

"I've never seen this side of you, Cole," Arohn declared. "And all it took to delight you was a few broken bones."

"Okay, Okay," Cole said and clicked the control again, bringing up the real-time feed from an interrogation room where Sauhn Lin was being questioned by two agents.

"This guy is the head of maintenance on the fixed telescope observatory. Ben Ru is his boss. As tough as Sauhn Lin looks, he's in there telling us everything he knows, which is a lot. He's given us a list of their cohorts, both here and back on The Planets. Ben Ru and Sauhn Lin are Copies, as are some of their associates. I suspect that their Originals remain on The Planets. Sauhn Lin claims that he and Ben Ru have been operating here under orders originally issued by O'Ruhn and BarOak, and that their goal is to eventually take control of the Mission."

Cole turned to Maritou. "We are ready to start transmitting this information to Hogar. What do you think?"

"Yes, send everything as it unfolds. Don't wait for my approval. And the DNA evidence on Sauhn Lin and Ben Ru?"

"It's being analyzed, and we'll have results, later today."

"What are you considering regarding arrests of their accomplices?" Maritou asked.

"Our resources are stretched pretty thin, right now," Cole noted. "We are sending agents to plant bugs, hoping to find out what their plans are. We want to recruit the help of the Armada Police but, first, we want to check the extent of infiltration. We don't know who to trust."

"Let's concentrate our efforts on countering possible terrorist activities," Maritou ordered. "Take an immediate inventory of all weapons and explosives. And direct questions to Sauhn Lin as to how radical he thinks any of their associates happen to be."

Cole picked up the remote, again. "These are the original clearance documents for Ben Ru and Sauhn Lin. They implicate several others, most of whom have prominent positions, here on the Mission. This corroborates the information being obtained from Sauhn Lin."

"Okay, good," Maritou said. "And what is the intel regarding their communication capabilities? I'm talking about their communications with The Planets."

"According to Sauhn Lin, they know about the Quantum Radio and have their own version in development. But, for now, they're still restricted to light-speed radio signals."

"And do you believe he is telling the truth?"

"Yes, and we think that is why Ben Ru didn't have Dar assassinated long ago. According to Sauhn Lin, Dar's husband asked BarOak to issue a hands-off order to protect her. Ben Ru might have been waiting for new orders from Hogar."

"Why did Ben Ru go to see Dar in the first place?" Maritou wondered.

"He saw her unexpectedly when they happened to be sharing a shuttle ride, and he thought she recognized him. From then on, they have kept her under surveillance. They tracked her to her interview with you, and well—Ben Ru decided to move against you."

"I would like to interview Sauhn Lin, myself," Maritou stated. "There is a good chance he has information helpful for Rena's rescue. Do we know his connection with Ben Ru prior to joining the Armada?"

"He says Ben Ru recruited him as his personal body guard back in the early days when they were both involved in slave trading. He also says that Ben Ru's real name is Sy Morah.

"Yes, I need to talk to him straight away."

Maritou sat with the chief interrogation officer. On the other side of the glass, Sauhn Lin's face was drawn, and his eyes had lost their shine.

"He looks tired," she observed. "Let's stop the interview here and get him something to eat. Let him stretch his legs a bit before I go in there."

Maritou took her own break before returning to the interrogation room. She entered, alone, and Sauhn Lin sat up quickly, in surprise.

"It's you!" He exclaimed, and pulled back against the tether, eyes wide.

"The restraint is there for your protection, not mine. I haven't come here to harm you. I just want to talk." she assured him.

The stiffness in his spine softened, and he slowly sat back in his chair. His fears were being replaced by his enchantment with this marvelous creature before him.

"You and Ben Ru go back a long time," she began.

"Why yes, we do."

"Tell me how you first met. What was it that made your association work?"

She refrained from going directly to her key questions, which might arouse his suspicions. She would try to get him to relax into their conversation. If he started talking about himself and she seemed interested, this might seem to be less of an interrogation, and he would open up more.

"Well, we met when I was leading a crew of slavers. We were rounding up a shipment of Abarus from an isolated island. Ben Ru arrived in his transport vessel to take possession. When I first saw him, he was standing at the makeshift loading dock that the Abarus, themselves, had constructed for us."

Sauhn continued. "Ben Ru was confused when he arrived to find the Abaru, unchained and waiting to voluntarily board a ship that would surely take them to their deaths. I explained to him that brutality was not necessary. Not a soul on the island had been killed or mistreated. We had tricked them by offering a solution to their problem of overcrowding. We agreed to take whole families to virgin islands in exchange for the rare gems that are produced by the Star Flower plant that only grows at that low altitude."

"He must have been impressed," Maritou noted.

"Yes! He promoted me to a new position. I became second in command of all the slavers and charged with revising the entire supply chain, from capture to final disposition. As long as the product was alive, it was my job to keep it in peak condition.

"My top priority became quality control for 'O'Ruhn's Virgins.' Prior to my modifications, cargo would arrive damaged or even useless. And, before there was 'Life Blood,' only immortal flesh could sustain the Vulan population to survive on Hogar."

He didn't need to tell Maritou that the Abaru, like all Gentar, quickly start to lose their immortality when mistreated.

Maritou, unable to hide her disgust, softened it somewhat so as not to break whatever trust existed between her and her captive. "It never bothered you that you were dealing with innocent lives?"

"I try not to dwell on it."

"I'm guessing that you are able to take that attitude for the same reason that you are now condemning your comrades."

He ruminated on that a bit before responding. "Yes, I think you are right. The Abarus' fate was sealed. It wasn't my choice. Someone else would have done it, had I not. And the same is true for Ben Ru and the others. They're going down anyway, so why not help myself?"

Noting that Sauhn liked to talk about himself, Maritou saw her chance to get the information she really wanted. If she made her questions about him, maybe he would not get suspicious of her motives.

"I'm curious."

"Yes?"

"You mentioned 'O'Ruhn's Virgins'—How did you deliver them into his hands without alarming them as to their fate?"

Sauhn sat up even more and smiled. "That was my crowning achievement. The key was that I made sure the Abaru felt like they had their freedom."

"And how did you do that?"

"Well, parts of O'Ruhn's ship had to be modified. The receiving dock had previously led to small holding cells. I had these remodeled into comfortable open chambers that were luxuriously appointed. The finest food and sleeping accommodations were provided. Their families were allowed to be with them for their short stay. They were all told that this vessel was the final transport taking them to their new home."

"And, what really happened to them?"

"Everything was a deception. A long corridor connected them to baths, where they went daily. Unknown to them, these baths had passageways to pleasure salons and to O'Ruhn's Ceremonial Chamber. When their time came, O'Ruhn's minions would come and lead groups of them into the clutches of the awaiting pleasure seekers or, most often, two or three at a time to O'Ruhn or BarOak."

Maritou continued to contain her true feelings. "This was all very clever of you. Your designs sound interesting. Do you think you could draw a floor plan?"

"Surely!"

She called for writing materials and had the guards remove Sauhn's restraints.

He began, straight away, working in the long, sure strokes of a natural artist, adding details as they returned to his memory.

She had to admit that he was quite handsome, intelligent, talented—and without a scruple.

Finally, he stopped and held up his finished work, savoring every pencil stroke before presenting it to his supposed admirer.

Perhaps it was his need for approval that had always guided him. He turned his artwork toward Maritou and laid it before her like a treasure.

She studied the drawing and then pointed to one side.

"So, this is the receiving dock—and these are the Abaru living quarters?"

"Yes."

"What are these small rooms behind each chamber?"

"That is where guards would sit undetected and have a full view of our guests."

"Okay. And this must be the corridor and the baths. What is this room at the far end?"

"It's a security surveillance room. The virgins, both male and female, would file past it on their way from the baths to the party rooms. This was manned, full time to secure this route, because the party rooms are connected to O'Ruhn's private suites.

"And this small room at the side of the baths?"

"That's where O'Ruhn would come watch the virgins and select his favorites. Whenever he wanted, he or his minions, would open a door to the baths and usher them through another passageway to his private chambers. Sometimes he would find a special one and have him or her brought to his Ceremonial Room, here," he explained, pointing to the corresponding parts of his drawing.

"I don't see a guardroom next to this passageway," she observed.

"No, there wasn't space to provide a separate guardroom and, with the surveillance room just a few steps away, it wasn't considered necessary."

"I don't see a supply closet here in the baths," Maritou noted.

"Oh! I forgot to draw that. It's here next to the passageway. The maintenance crew would bring the supplies through an elevator, here in the main corridor when they came to clean."

Maritou believed that she now had the information she needed, and she was formulating a plan in her mind.

"Thank you for your cooperation. Our talk has been very interesting."

His face sagged. "You remind me of someone," he said, his voice resonating from a place deep in his chest." He did not want her to leave.

"I do?"

"You remind me of Miah, one of O'Ruhn's minions. I have never doubted that she loved me. But it couldn't last. I should have known that."

Maritou felt a strange tinge of compassion for her would-be killer.

"You still love her."

"That will never end"

"I must go now, Sauhn Lin. I do hold out some hope for you," she revealed. "I'm sure you will be treated mercifully."

She rolled up the drawing and headed to the Communication Center to contact Hogar.

Venahus was close to the radio when Maritou called.

"How are things at your end?" Number II asked her.

"Well, we've decided not to delay Rena's rescue. The supply ship is scheduled for tomorrow, so we are going in then. Otherwise, we'll have to wait fifteen days for the next shipment."

Venahus's voice sounded like it was coming from the other side of the desk. Thanks to quantum entanglement, it had instantly crossed the one hundred and fifty light years from Hogar to the Armada.

"I've just sent you a drawing I obtained from my interview with Sauhn Lin. Do you have it?"

"Yes, it's right here."

Maritou briefed her Original on what she had learned.

"Looks like the supply closet would be a good entry point. If someone could pose as one of the maintenance crew, they could try to smuggle one or two rescuers in a supply cart and get them into the closet without being detected. From there they could breach the wall and get into the passageway."

"Good thinking. Without this, and the other information you've gathered, we would be flying blind."

"The hardest part, on this end, will be waiting while you are out of communication," Number II said.

"Just go and take care of Gar—Take care of each other."

Chapter 12

Fabric of Space

Gar's head had a light bandage to cover the open wound. The tremendous headache he'd felt earlier, had turned into a faint throbbing.

"I'm starving," he told Maritou.

"How did I know that?" she laughed. "There are only two times when you aren't hungry."

"Well, I'm not sleeping and you haven't made any moves on me—yet."

"That might happen if you're not careful. Your bandage is starting to turn me on."

She ran her hand over his face and kissed him softly.

"I was so frightened when I found you, bleeding in the lab. I thought for a moment . . ."

"That I was dead? But think of all the fun you could have while I was being duplicated," he tried to joke but noticed that Maritou's mood had turned serious.

He changed the subject. "What news have you brought on Rena's rescue?"

"Time has run out. They go in tomorrow. We've done all we can do to help from here."

"The mission plan is still Maritou and Arohn?"

"Yes, and Sten. The rescue team will be observing radio silence. All we can do now is wait."

With this, Gar felt a surge of acid reaching his esophagus. But, this time he did not avoid his unpleasant emotions and took a small step toward intimacy.

"I confess," he revealed, "that, ever since we received news that Rena is alive and may be rescued, I've buried myself in our work, trying to drown out my thoughts."

Maritou took Gar's water glass and began her ritual of small sips; the only thing that might bring a measure of calm. That, and belly breathing. Gentars were like humans in that way. It is impossible to have a panic attack if one is breathing properly.

"Are you okay?"

"Yes," she lied, blocking a chance for intimacy, "it's just that I haven't eaten, today."

Now was not the time to confess the fears she had been having. There would be time for that, once Rena's fate became known.

"We have some leftovers," Gar said, heading for the kitchen.

He returned with two plates and held her chair as she joined him.

Actually, she discovered that she really was hungry, and the leftovers went down easily.

"I'm having a hard time, myself, shutting down my thoughts," she confided.

"Why don't we talk about the saucer?" Gar suggested.

"Yes. I'll be busy, after tonight, working with Cole's security team. We may not have much time after this, and I would like to share my most recent ideas with you."

"Please do."

"Well, I have made a few assumptions about the relationship between matter and space."

"Yes?" Gar coaxed.

"Assumption number one is that space rules inertia. That is, it is space itself that holds an object in its current state of velocity, or lack of velocity relative to its position in space; and every point in space is unique. Space can be void of matter, but it still has a fabric. It is not empty, and at the very least, contains a force field. Perhaps as space expands, the forces of inertia lessen and allow light photons, or even solid objects, to move faster. Maybe it is inertia that is being stretched and not actually space that is expanding. For our purposes, it may not matter."

"I hadn't thought of that," he declared.

"Assumption number two is that solid objects retain their size, shape and mass no matter how much the space that they occupy might expand. Space does not determine these qualities."

Although Gar held similar beliefs, he simply said, "I'm following you."

"Given that," she continued, "and assuming my solid object assumption is correct, an object will tend to be deformed and pulled apart as space warp moves through it. But if the object is flexible enough to take a given amount of warp, it can emerge in good condition."

"Interesting." Gar exclaimed. "This interfaces with what I have been doing in the lab. The other day, I was in front of a cooling fan that came on automatically. At first, I felt no air movement. It took time for the pressure to reach me but, when it did, it seemed to hit me all at once with a steady stream of air. So I made my own hypothesis."

Gar rubbed the lump on his head. "I was getting ready to test my theory when everything went black. Anyway, I think my experiment will support my assumption that space expands in ways similar to a gas, like wind pressure generated by a fan. Maybe we can modify the experiment and use it to test your ideas about solid matter."

"I have an idea," Maritou suggested. "Do you feel well enough to go to the weightless lab and run some tests?"

"Okay, that's better than staying here waiting and worrying."

The weightless lab was cold when Gar and Maritou came in out of the airlock. Gar switched on the heat lamps while Maritou started the air filtration system to remove the dried droplets of blood that floated all about.

"We'll have to send in a cleaning crew to really clean this place up," she remarked, noticing the splatters on the walls.

"Let's have some music," Gar suggested and went to a control panel. He selected a piece with a smooth rhythm, long notes, and crescendos. It was a favorite of theirs and they couldn't resist. They had discovered, years earlier that they both enjoyed improvisational dance. They had not done this before in weightless conditions.

Maritou flew to the middle of the lab, dramatically pretending to escape a pursuer. In harmony with a suspenseful and sinister phrase in the composition, Gar slowly crept forward, as if stalking his prey. When the music burst into a set of accented chords, he sprang upon her. In and out they struggled until, exhausted, the victim gave up, exposing her tender parts willingly to her attacker. She had him in her trap!

They laughed and laughed. It was one of their best performances. It was flawless!

"Shall we do some science, now?"

"Might as well. We can't top that," Gar said.

He went to the equipment locker and removed a set of rods. "I have all the equipment ready for placement," he told her.

She began fastening the rods together, end to end.

Gar pulled out a smaller version of the Hidden Energy generator and fastened it to its wall mount and attached the rod assembly to it.

"Now, while you place the sensors along the rod, I'll set up the rest of the gear," Gar said. "I'm sure you can see, from the setup, how this experiment will go. Much of it is a scaled-down version of our original experiment, except it will measure the speed of laser beams at different intervals of distance and time."

They tested the speed of the light beams to check the sensors and to calibrate the speedometer without firing the Hidden Energy gun.

"Check, and check," Gar declared when the standard readings were confirmed.

He turned on the generator.

"Huh!" Maritou sighed in disappointment. The thrum of the tiny generator was too weak to send delicious sensations through her body.

Gar hovered in front of the control panel. "I'll run the test several times and, each time, I'll change the timing of the light to coincide with the firing of the gun."

After several tests were completed, they huddled together at the computer screen and waited while the results were run through a program, converting the data into tables and graphs.

Gar was behind her, resting his chin on her shoulder.

"I know what you want," she teased.

"It's amazing how you can read me," he quirked merrily.

Somehow, they managed to divert their attention to the monitor.

"Wow!" she exclaimed, as she studied the results. "This is undeniable support for your hypothesis. It's as if a wall of expanding space moves out from the energy source and, like your wind analogy, it moves out like a wave and seems to be absorbed into the ambient space, losing its power the further out it goes."

"And I think there is enough data here to calculate the speed of the expansion effect, which is clearly much slower than the speed of light," Gar noted.

"Yes, I thought so. And that slowness is a positive factor for practical applications." Maritou stated. "It allows the expansion to build up close to the energy source without having to increase the amount of energy being supplied. Take the saucer, for example. The expansion build-up next to the bottom, which is a less curved surface, would be greater than the build-up next to the more curved surface at the top, assuming equal amounts of energy to both surfaces. The craft, even if otherwise motionless, will be carried along in the space it occupies—kind of like a cork floating on a stream—a stream of space.

"And, as you told me before," Gar added, "it is irrelevant how far out from the surfaces the expansion extends. The intensity of the expansion right next to the surfaces is the only thing that matters. Since space acts like a gas, the expansion, further away from the surface, will mix rapidly with the surrounding ambient space."

"And the process of expansion is going on constantly, throughout the Universe," Maritou said. "As stars burn, galaxies are emitting huge amounts of Hidden Energy, causing expansion and pushing the galaxies further apart."

"There is so much we don't know," Observed Gar. "But we are learning fast."

"Hmm! Maritou declared. "I just thought of a way to test one of my assumptions. Give me a moment."

She went to the first aid kit and opened it.

"This will do."

She broke off a piece of the foam packing and took it to the rod assembly, measured it carefully, and tied it to the sensor bracket closest to the Hidden Energy gun.

"Okay, Let's fire the gun a few times. This foam should be flexible but will not spring back into shape. If it expands, it should stay expanded.

They fired the gun several times and she took the measurements, again.

"Oh! Beatle juice and bug sauce!" She cried. "No change."

She started to untie the foam, disappointed.

"Wait!" Gar shouted. "Let's try something."

He made some adjustments at the control panel. He fired the gun and made more adjustments, repeating the process a few times.

"I really don't think you need to measure," he said. "Just watch the foam."

He touched a button on the control panel and the foam grew larger before their eyes!

"What did you do?"

"I simply increased the duration of the blast, allowing the expansion to build until it reached enough intensity to stretch the foam."

"I should be happy, I guess," she reflected. "But this presents us with serious problems. The saucer, and everything inside, will need to be sufficiently rubbery to survive the space warp."

"But you suspected this already. I saw your drawing of the space man. He looked pretty rubbery."

"That was a drawing of you going back to Rena!" she lashed out, unexpectedly.

Tears welled up and she clutched him, cheek to cheek, attempting to hide her eyes. Her flippant barb had turned on her.

"You don't believe, for a moment, that I would ever abandon you," he soothed.

"No, no. I'm just being silly. It's probably the stress of everything that's happening."

He gently wiped away the teardrops with his thumbs and kissed her softly on the lips.

"You don't know what you mean to me," he asserted.

"Just hold me."

She wondered to herself, *If I hold on tight enough . . . can anything last forever?*

Wrapped in her sleeping bag, Maritou awoke to the sensation of falling. She attempted to use her wings until she realized where she was.

Years ago, the first time she had slept over in the weightless lab, she and Gar had fastened their bags together. They spent a sleepless night thrashing around, only to discover that every movement would disturb the other. Not only that, but without the use of their wings, making love in weightlessness was practically impossible.

Cramped in the bag, releasing muscle tension in the wings was proving difficult. And her mind was racing from one thought to the next.

The idea of childbirth swept in unexpectedly. Embedded in the walls of her womb, she harbored the semen from the first time she opened her inner sex organs to Gar. It would remain there, dormant, until the time she would choose to use it or to expel it from her body.

Why have we waited? We've discussed this on many occasions. And each time, as much as we want a child, we decide that the time is not right. Have we just been lying to ourselves? Is our love as strong as I believed it to be?

A list of seemingly valid reasons had emerged over the years. There was Gar's responsibility as co-commander of the mission; there was their scientific work that may prove critical to the mission's success; and then, there was their shared fear of parenting in the environment of the Armada.

A few of their friends had had children during the mission. "The Newborns" their children were called.

Whether they were Gentar or Vulan, the Newborns tended to band together in their own separate culture and disconnect from their parents and from the Mission.

These reasons all make sense. But are we conveniently hiding the possibility that maybe we have unspoken doubts about our relationship? How could Gar love me as much as Rena? She's so much better than I.

At this, her body temperature shot up and she quickly unzipped the bag, releasing herself to the chill of the open lab. It felt exhilarating, though, and she stretched her wings wide from tip to tip as her lungs filled and contracted.

She observed Gar's bag. She could hear the peaceful sound of his breathing.

He can always sleep, no matter what. And he wakes in high spirits. I hate him! She chuckled.

Returning to her own bag, she fastened it loosely, just enough to warm her a bit and keep her from floating back out. But she still could not slip into that delicious twilight state that could shield her from her runaway thoughts—from her fears.

Well, we will find out soon. And then what? I don't believe Gar realizes how much his feelings might change. I know he feels steadfast in our relationship now, but whether or not Rena survives, will he enter a new stage of his grief over her loss? Will his urge to run to her overpower his love for me? If she dies, he may no longer feel that restoring her would be a betrayal. But how can I begin to really understand his grief? I cannot! And maybe it has been my inevitable misunderstanding that has bolstered my fears.

She called out to the Powers of Creation, to the omnipotent driving force of the Universe. *I don't want to lose him. Please! Please allow me the strength to endure whatever comes.*

The answer came, but it was far from the one she had expected. It came in a flood of compassion for Gar. Not for herself, for once, and she wept uncontrollably for him.

My dear sweet love! How you must have suffered!

This shift of focus, from herself, changed her forever. The years of resentment and shame, both of which she had felt but never acknowledged, were evaporating.

If the worst comes to pass, I think I can forgive him.

A tremendous weight had been lifted and she drifted into a nourishing sleep. She wouldn't realize it, until later, but the release of resentments she had just experienced, would now make room for other changes in her life.

Chapter 13

Whole New Ballgame

Stepping from his home on the island of Mon Mari, Sten was on his way to rendezvous with Venahus and le Noir for the rescue mission. Three military policemen stopped him at the doorstep. He was being detained for questioning, the one with the razor-thin face informed him.

A short time, later, the police vehicle arrived at what looked like a prison facility. He was escorted through a busy reception room and down a hallway. As they approached the far end, a door opened and an orderly emerged, pushing a gurney. The orderly and his lifeless cargo disappeared down a side corridor.

As the door was closing, Sten glimpsed what looked like an operating table equipped with restraints.

Just before they reached the dreaded door, his escorts directed him into a room on the right with a table and three chairs. Behind the table was a door that undoubtedly led into their chamber of fun.

"Sit!" demanded one of the officers. There were now only two; Razor face and the husky one—Grif and Karn. Sten had picked up on his abductor's names on the short journey from his home.

Grif took a chair across from Sten and donned a concerned look. Sten surmised that Grif was the one in charge and, definitely, the more intelligent of the two.

Karn, meanwhile, disappeared through the ominous door at Sten's back. As the door closed, the faint odor of urine and feces seeped into the room.

If they are trying to frighten me, they're doing a good job. However this unfolds, I must stay calm.

Karn returned. He glared menacingly as he paced the room.

"I'm sure you know that your old schoolboy companion, Rayloh Cari has disappeared." Grif stated in a concerned tone.

"Yes, I think the whole world knows that." Sten answered sarcastically.

"When was the last time you spoke to your friend?"

Karn stopped pacing just behind Sten, who felt his hot breath.

Grif frowned at Karn and waved him away.

"Rayloh is not my friend. But I did see him at the Worldwide Science Symposium not long ago."

"You had an argument with him, didn't you?" Karn demanded.

"You think I had something to do with his disappearance?"

"And, what do you know about his disappearance?" Karn continued.

"Why nothing! I certainly didn't kill him. I figured it was your bosses that had gotten rid of him. He's been a thorn in their asses for a long time."

Grif changed the subject. "Your argument with him was over Naomi Kamara, wasn't it? You were both interested in the same woman?"

Sten didn't bother answering.

"And, before the end of the Symposium, you went to see Maritou Venahus in her hotel room."

"Yes, I did."

"You have a thing for Rayloh's women, don't you?" Karn sneered.

Sten felt a stirring of anger. *But why hide the truth, even from these thugs. And maybe Karn is giving me an irreproachable motive for my meeting with Maritou.*

Sten looked directly at Grif when he replied to Karn's barb. "I won't deny what is true. I've loved Maritou since I was a boy."

"So, if you can't have Naomi, you'll settle for Maritou." Karn goaded.

"That's not the reason why I went to see her."

Grif motioned to Karn to ease up.

"Okay, tell us," said Grif.

"Well, she and Rayloh had broken up a few years ago. I know how much she adored him, and I went to see how she was doing. Anyway, Maritou is my friend."

"Don't you think she's a little sick for bedding down with a mere youngster?" Karn continued to jab.

"No, I don't." Sten said flatly.

Karn was livid. Try as he might, he couldn't rattle his prey. "We're wasting time, here!" Karn burst out in frustration. He wanted to see Sten strapped to the table, next door.

"Go and get us something to drink." Grif scolded.

Karn didn't have the clearance for what Grif had to discuss, next. Since the time of the reign of the despot, Lu Mah, who ruled for 500 years after the launch of the Armada, the mention of Vulans, or even the Mission, was forbidden. Except for the legends that survived in Gentar mythology, the general population knew nothing of these things, and Karn was among the ignorant.

Grif made a hand signal toward the cameras and a surveillance officer switched the live feed and the recordings to top secret mode. Little did they know that le Noir had hacked into their systems, long ago.

"And, what can you tell me of Arohn le Noir? Grif asked abruptly.

This time, Grif's smile, that had disguised its cold-blooded owner, turned to a sinister snarl.

"Who?"

Grif hesitated, studying Sten's reaction.

Sten's heart raced.

"You deny knowing him?"

"I've never heard of him."

"He's a Vulan."

"I don't know many Vulans," Sten said flatly, getting into the rhythm of lying. "The only ones I've seen were on my father's ship."

"You are lying! I can smell it! But anyway, it doesn't matter. Your father will deal with you now. Tonight, you will be transported for a little family reunion. From what I've heard, there is no love lost between you and your dad. He wants the pleasure of extracting the truth out of you."

Chapter 14

Tit for Tat

Something was pulling Maritou from a deep slumber. Her and Gar's portables were ringing at the same time. She checked the screen. It was Lore Li.

"Maritou here."

Lore Li's voice was rushed and reached a high pitch. "Sten has been arrested!"

"What?"

"We don't have many details, but the mission has been scuttled."

"And the rest of the team?" Maritou asked.

"They were on the way to the supply depot to meet up with Sten when le Noir got word of his arrest. They are all safe, back at field command."

Maritou overheard Gar swearing and questioning de Vul on his portable.

"We are in the weightless lab." Maritou told Lore Li. "We'll be at the Command Center as soon as we can get there.

"Maritou? There's something else. Cole and de Vul want a meeting with you as soon as possible. Ben Ru has woken up and is starting to talk."

"We'll leave here straight away."

*   *   *

Maritou and de Vul met with Cole in a small office in Security Head-quarters. This time it was just the three of them.

Cole played them a video clip from Ben Ru's hospital room. Ben Ru was sitting up in bed, glaring at the camera. He appeared to be alone.

"You'll all be dead soon!" He ranted. "Mihn Rova will take you out! You have no idea…"

Two orderlies appeared on camera, summoned by the rapid changes in Ben Ru's monitor readings. He thrashed at them, tearing loose his I.V. tubes.

Cole clicked off the video.

"Unfortunately, that's all we have," Cole told them. "He's fully awake now, and refuses to tell us more. He doesn't acknowledge saying the things he did while in his semi-conscious state."

"Do we know anything about what or who Mihn Rova happens to be?" Maritou asked.

"Well, there is only one person with that name that has ever been in living form on the Armada. I happen to know her," Cole revealed. "She's an entomologist—a Gentar. It's been many years since I've seen her, but I cannot believe she would involve herself in a plot with traitors. She has an impeccable record and is in charge of a small but elite group. She has made many valuable contributions to the Mission. But there is a lot more to the story and it is disturbing."

"Yes?"

"She's a copy. Her original disappeared without a trace a couple of centuries ago. We've looked for her everywhere—nothing."

"She has never been found," Arohn joined in, "and I ordered her replication not long after Cole ran out of leads."

"I'd like to turn this over to you, Maritou." Cole proposed. "We suspect that Mihn Rova's original is still alive and developing technologies for the conspirators. We need your fresh and unique perspective."

Maritou took some time to respond. "Okay," She declared, finally. "I'll need to absorb all the information you have on her and her disappearance. Then, we'll talk about the next step."

Cole handed her a set of memory pearls. "Here's everything we have on Mihn Rova; interviews with her copy, her background, her associates, her disappearance, her copy's subsequent history—everything."

"Good. And I'll need your files on all known conspirators," Maritou added.

"Do you know what would happen if you are taken captive?" de Vul warned.

"Yes," she responded without hesitation. "And, I'll prepare myself to do what needs to be done if that happens. I'll go from this meeting to get my memory crystalized, just in case."

"And, your body guards will not be far away," Arohn promised. "Agreed?"

"Agreed."

"We have offices ready for you here in Security," Cole told her. "I knew you would accept the assignment."

"I know where your office is," Arohn offered. "Let me walk you over."

De Vul gave Maritou the quick tour of her two adjoining rooms. They were fully equipped with the latest electronic devices. There were several surveillance monitors that could pick up live or recorded feed from any of the thousands of cameras throughout the Armada. He showed her the weapons locker which already contained all of her own armaments and a variety of modern instruments designed for killing or disabling an opponent, as well as restraining devices.

She registered surprise at seeing her own weaponry, which had not been touched by anyone but her, for centuries.

"Gar gathered them and brought them over. I hope you don't mind."

"No," she told him, relieved, knowing it was Gar. "I'm glad to have it all here."

Arohn's mood turned suddenly dark, like a storm rolling in, quietly, but ready to burst into a deluge or shoot forth bolts of fire.

"Arohn!" Maritou reacted with alarm. "What has happened?"

His tear ducts erupted into fountains. Maritou took his out-stretched hands as he reached for her support. She pulled him into her arms and embraced him as the spasms of his breath slowly subsided.

"The DNA!" he choked, surprising himself by the magnitude of the feelings that had lain dormant since the loss of his cherished partner.

Maritou realized he referred to the results of the genetic analysis of Ben Ru and Sauhn Lin. She helped him to one of the tall chairs placed there for Lore Li and other Vulan team members.

He sighed deeply, his breathing slowly returning to normal.

"Ben Ru's DNA is a positive match, but Sauhn Lin's is not," Arohn told her. "When Cole told me, I knew I needed to talk to you. And, at that moment, I realized how isolated I have been from my own kind. Other than Lore Li, the three people that mean the most to me are all Gentar."

Maritou did not ask what he planned to do with Ben Ru. Under the Constitution, such matters were to fall back to original Vulan or Gentar laws and customs. As such, Ben Ru's fate was totally in the hands of the injured husband. Arohn was silent regarding Ben Ru's final reckoning, and Maritou supposed that he would consider his options with much intention.

"I think that was all I needed," Arohn said. "I adore you, Maritou! I know you are always there for me."

"Always!"

"Shall I send Lore Li over?" Arohn asked.

"I need to get my bearings, first. And, right now, I think I should check on Gar."

In another part of the galaxy, Sten was handcuffed to Karn in the backseat of the air shuttle ride to the transport that would take him to O'Ruhn's flagship. Security officers monitored the flight via a camera in the cabin. Halfway into the short hop to their destination, the security monitor showed a sudden jolt and then went dark. When it came back online, they saw Sten jumping out of the craft as it spiraled toward the island.

Minutes later, Karn and the pilot were pulled from the wreckage, unconscious.

One of the wings had been sheared off of the shuttle in a mid-air collision. Witnesses said that the other craft went down beyond the edge of the island. Recovering it would be impossible unless it happened to have crashed into another island floating beneath Mon Mari.

But there were several details that the camera had missed. At the moment of impact, le Noir's marksmen fired non-lethal rounds, taking out Karn and the pilot just as the camera was temporarily taken off line. The rest was an unchoreographed ballet, as a Gentar who looked and dressed a lot like Sten entered the spinning craft and freed its prisoner. He told Sten to disappear below the island and then literally pushed him out. The camera came back on and captured footage of the imposter making his escape.

Chapter 15

Vernah Berry Wine

After a brief reunion and meal with Gar, Maritou returned to her new office and immersed herself in the intelligence files. She found them to be well organized and indexed.

The life and illustrious career of Mihn Rova came to life as Maritou studied the otherwise dry and sterile files. She watched the taped interviews, and was getting a real sense of Mihn's character. Without a doubt, this woman would not have gone willingly into the service of terrorists.

Many of the interviews had been conducted by Cole himself. As the interviews progressed, they demonstrated an increasing trust, and even friendship, between Mihn and Cole.

Do I detect a growing attraction? Maritou wondered.

Maritou met with Cole, the next day, to formulate her next move.

"I'd like a face to face with Mihn Rova. Maybe we can do that without drawing attention to her," Maritou suggested.

"What are you thinking?" asked Cole.

"Well, as far as we know, the conspirators have no idea that Ben Ru has unwittingly divulged her name to us. They also have no reason to believe that she could supply us with any fresh leads after being so thoroughly questioned in the past.

"I agree with you, there. They probably have no eyes on her anymore."

"We can't bring her in for an interview. Can you get a message to her?" Maritou asked.

"That shouldn't be a problem."

"I have the feeling that she can be trusted."

"I'm sure she can," Cole agreed.

"Her apartment is the logical choice," Maritou suggested. "We would have no time constraints and be able to avoid detection, once I am inside."

"I'll set it up," Cole assured her.

Later, that day, this note was handed to Mihn Rova by a supply worker:

Mihn,

Destroy this note as soon as you have read it. We would like another interview with you, this time, in secret. The most secure place would be in your apartment. If you agree, signal affirmative by carrying some work to take home when you leave the office this evening.

Someone will be waiting, inside, when you reach your apartment. Be careful.

– Cole

To signal her agreement, Mihn left her laboratory toting a briefcase. Arriving home, she opened the door and proceeded to the next room, where a light was on.

Maritou stood, as the tall and stately Gentar came in.

"I'm Maritou le Rohn. Thank you for meeting with me, in this unusual manner."

"You don't need to apologize. Col. BeCholn's note made it clear that secrecy is important," said Mihn, as she took Maritou's hand.

"Please call me Mihn. Let me bring us some refreshments."

"By all means. Can I help?"

Mihn's kitchen was well equipped and immaculate, other than a few breakfast dishes waiting in the sink.

Mihn passed Maritou a handful of long narrow leaves, which Maritou had not seen before.

"Here, you can toast these Williper Leaves while I whip up a dip to put on them."

Next, she brought out a bowl full of bean-like seeds and put them through a grinder, turning them into a thick paste, releasing their delicate odor.

"Those are Wa Wa pods, aren't they?"

"Yes."

"I love them. What a treat."

Mihn added some spices, salt, and a shot of a dark wine she had made from Vernah Berries. Showing the bottle to Maritou, she asked, "Would you partake in some of this?"

"Why not?"

"Let's go sit in the dining room."

The pair took their time enjoying the finger food and wine while they became acquainted.

"You know," said Mihn, "I'm always so busy with my work, I have no social life to speak of. I'm really enjoying this."

"I am too. Cole did not tell me how welcoming you are."

"How is Cole?" Mihn's voice hung on at the end of her question.

"You and Cole have a special relationship, don't you?"

"We did. But, you know, we both have our work."

So much was revealed in this simple exchange, that Maritou felt a wave of empathy and inhaled, slowly. Later, when she was alone, she did not hold back the tears for her new friend.

"Anyway," Mihn said, changing the subject, "you have things you want to discuss—and I want to help."

Maritou held out her empty wine cup and smiled at Mihn.

Mihn gave a little chuckle and poured each of them more wine.

"Well, I came here mostly to learn more about your work," Maritou began. "You have already answered plenty of questions about the details leading up to—how shall I say it—your disappearance? Maybe you can start by giving me a history of how your work has evolved from the beginning of the Mission?"

"Okay—well, it started years before the launch. I was initially trained as a lab assistant. We were tackling the problem of organic waste. It was a major obstacle to the viability of the Mission. It was realized, early on, that it wouldn't take long for garbage to take over. We couldn't just throw it out into outer space because it is a precious resource."

"And, then it was you, yourself, that came up with a breakthrough," Maritou prompted, gently guiding the subject matter.

"It was a team effort really, and there were several breakthroughs. I had the wonderful experience of working with many brilliant scientists and engineers.

"One of the biggest problems was the buildup of methane," Mihn continued. "The Vulans already had advanced technologies to deal with toxic amounts of CO_2. They needed to because the atmospheric pressure on Vul's surface was slowly falling as the gases constantly eroded from the solar wind. They took to living underground in pressurized lava tubes and caves and they had to find a solution to the buildup of CO_2. They had a lesser problem with methane produced in composting because they out-gassed it through their ventilation process. Here, of course, we can't do that because it would slowly deplete our supply of hydrogen and carbon.

"Anyway, another group had developed the portable methane wand. And I started carrying mine everywhere and used it to measure the methane levels in and around anything that crossed my path. It was when I took it on vacation to my old home on Hogar, that I discovered something interesting. The methane levels, around bubble plants, is significantly lower than anywhere else in the Hogar atmosphere."

"What happened, then?"

"My supervisors gave me a promotion and a transfer to work with a botany research lab on Hogar. We soon discovered that the bubble plant has the unique ability to obtain some of its carbon from methane. It actually prefers methane to CO_2. With that, we developed a hybrid that is smaller. It gobbles up methane but does not produce bubbles that block light and take up an unmanageable amount of space. As a bonus, almost any fruit can be grafted to it."

"So, what was the next phase in the evolution of your work?"

"It was after the launch. The Vulans decided to train me in genetic research; first in plants and then in animals. It turned out that, after years into the Mission, the food growers were losing the battle with crop destroying pests. Chemical interventions worked okay at first, but it became apparent that we were poisoning the environment and, at the same time, destroying the nutritional value of the produce.

"We concentrated, at first, on producing an abundance of pest killing insects. But their behavior isn't what one might expect. Instead of continuing to prey on the pests, they do what is in the best interest of their species in the long haul. They don't wipe out their food supply. Instead, they feed voraciously to a certain point, and then they change their behavior. They actually start protecting the pests from other predators and allow them to maintain significant numbers, enough to damage the crops. So, then came the Pestbot, which was totally a mechanical robotic system."

"Please tell me about the Rovabot," Maritou prompted. "The Pestbot was 100% effective, from what I've read. Why the need for Rovabot?"

"Maintenance," Mihn explained. "The Pestbot demanded a lot of resources to keep it operating efficiently. There were a lot of moving parts that wore out. And they needed batteries that eventually failed, and those were either difficult or impossible to recycle. But I think, the biggest incentive for the change were the complaints from the growers. They were expected to do most of the maintenance and this took them away from doing what they love—cultivating their crops.

"The Rovabots are living insects, genetically engineered to behave in specific ways. They do the majority of the maintenance themselves by reproducing and then dying. At a certain time in their lifecycle, they search out, what we call, 'a helmet'. They instinctively know how to don their helmet, which then controls where they go and what pests they will then search out and destroy. The helmet limits the amount of nutrition received for each kill so that they don't stop killing. And the helmet, which acts as a shield and has built-in weaponry, allows them to target pests that have chemical defenses or armored plates.

"When they reach their reproductive cycle," Mihn concluded, "they leave their helmets in special staging areas where a new generation can find them, easily. The helmets never wear out."

"Amazing!" Maritou marveled. "It seems that there is unlimited potential for this type of technology.

"Well, I thought a lot about that very thing as development progressed and I became very concerned. Because the potential of the technology for evil is so great, I decided to alert the Council. So I shared my fears with the only Council member that I knew at the time, Cli Oberdahn.

"Cli took my concerns to the Oversight Committee which, in turn, appointed a subcommittee to investigate. Soon, they were at my door and, to my chagrin, they hounded me half to death. They even formed another committee to have me investigated to see if I was fit to carry on with my work."

"Yes, I read that in your file."

"That committee recommended that I be removed and the project taken over by a scientist from the Solay Mahn Asteroid Array who was a brother of one of the senior Council members, the powerful Vulan, Mi Dulamar.

"What happened?"

"Well, the Council made its final decision, and I was on my way out. My reputation was tarnished and I had no assignments. Then de Vul stepped in. Actually, I'm still here under his executive order. But the damage had been done—Many in the scientific community still regard me with suspicion.

Maritou sat back and thought silently.

"Where do you get this wine?" she asked, finally.

Mihn laughed at the unexpected tension reducer.

"I ferment it from Vernah Berries," Mihn said, as she went for another bottle. "Come over sometime and we'll make some, together."

Mihn poured more wine.

"Let's make a list of everyone on those committees and anyone else connected," Maritou suggested.

Maritou wrote as Mihn called off the names she remembered and spoke of their involvement.

"Dulamar, himself, took a place on the committee that recommended my removal," Mihn noted. "He didn't have a lot to say during my interrogations, but I felt the tide shifting against me as soon as he came on board.

"Interesting," Maritou said, turning the page in her notebook. "I also want to make a list of the supplies and equipment you need in your work. If the conspirators have set up their own labs and production facilities, they will need the same things and we may be able to track the flow of shipments.

The two worked late into the night. Maritou would emerge with more lines of inquiry than she had suspected she would.

Toward the end, Maritou asked, "A few centuries have passed since you shared your concerns with Cli Oberdahn. Do you still have the same worries?"

Mihn leaned forward, with her elbows on the table, and pursed her lips tightly.

"I'm going to share something with you, Maritou."

Mihn rose from the table and crossed the room to a small desk. Reaching behind, she pulled a lever that released the desktop. Below, in the back was a shallow compartment. She pulled out a thick binder and returned to Maritou.

"These are plans for, what I have termed, the Defenderbot. It's designed to attack and kill swarms of insects that terrorists might use for assassinations. I've worked on it, in secret, for many years. Now, you are the only other person that knows. So, yes. I do have the same concerns.

"What would it take to get these into production?" Maritou wondered.

"From the design phase," Mihn said, holding up the plans, "to deployment of the final product—two or three years, normally."

"Normally?"

"Yes, but that would be unacceptable. So, I have worked out a quicker solution. Much quicker."

"How is that?"

"Well, for years now, I have been modifying the microchips used for all the different Rovabot helmets. They still do the same job of killing pests, but they are now capable of much, much more. And since it is routine to make design changes, I was able to do it undetected. I don't think anyone suspects what I have done."

Mihn went back to her secret compartment and pulled out a memory pearl.

"This contains alternate programs to use in the controller which sends commands to the helmets. All that is needed is to load these programs and select the desired instructions to the various Bots and, voila, you have an army of defenders at your fingertips. Any grower would have at least one spare controller.

Maritou sat, open-mouthed.

Mihn gave the pearl to Maritou. "You'll need swarming containers, and the bots equipped with helmets. You can obtain all of it from any grower. Cole will know which growers you can trust."

Mihn explained to Maritou how the controllers worked and gave her the passwords needed.

"Be very careful, Maritou, but if there are terrorists getting ready to strike, find them. And, I am here if you need me."

"Don't worry!" Maritou assured her. "Next time you see me, I'll be carrying a big bag of Vernah Berries."

Chapter 16

The Bean Counter

Coming from her meeting with Mihn, Maritou went directly to her new offices. She would sleep, later. First, she would set some things into play.

Cole wasn't at work yet, so she called Lore Li at the Command Center.

"Good morning, Lore Li."

"Maritou! Have you heard? Sten has been freed."

"You mean they let him go?"

"No. Arohn and Venahus devised a plan. They made it look like Sten escaped during an accident. The military believes that Sten was somehow involved in Rayloh and Naomi's disappearance, but they have no idea of the extent of Arohn and Maritou's involvement, nor that there is a plan to rescue Rena."

"Then the rescue plans remain in place. Wonderful!"

"Yes. We haven't received the details, yet, but we assume it will happen with the next supply shipment."

"Good. Right now, we have a few matters to address, here on the asteroids. I'm giving you top security clearance to work with me over here, if you agree."

"I am at your command. I'll clear it with Arohn. I'll be over, shortly."

Alone in her office, Maritou was longing for Gar and dialed his portable. He had been exercising—flying and weight training. He was heading for his bath. She loved the fragrance of his body right after exercise—musky, salty and with his unique spiciness.

"I miss you!" she growled.

"When will I see you?" he urged.

"I'm not sure at the moment but I'm going to need some sleep before too long and you can tuck me in—I've got to go. See you soon."

Cole appeared and, after a brief discussion of the situation back on Hogar, she summarized her meeting with Mihn.

"I need Lore Li's help on this, Cole. Any problem?"

"I knew you would, so, I've already upgraded her security clearance. Your adjoining office is ready for her."

"Thank you. Say, is Sauhn Lin still here? I want to interview him, again."

"Ah! We're keeping him here for now."

"And Cole, would you have one of your agents contact someone for me and arrange a meeting?"

"Of course! Who is it?"

"His name is Vin Pah Dumah. He's an accounting clerk for Lundah and Associates, the independent auditing firm. I have some data I want him to check."

"Don't you want someone with some credentials? This guy is only a clerk."

"That doesn't mean much. He's probably more competent than his bosses. I think they've held him back because of his social shortcomings. And, let's not let him know it is me that wants to see him. We don't want to arouse any suspicions with his employer. Today, after he gets off work, would be perfect, if it can be done."

Lore Li was waiting when Cole left and Maritou showed her the offices.

"This room will be yours, but they are almost identical, except that yours has more surveillance monitors."

"This will do me fine. What is my first assignment?"

Maritou gave her the list of names she and Mihn had compiled and briefed her on the objectives.

You have free reign, Lore Li, but I might suggest that you start by gathering the Council's committee reports involving Mihn Rova and any documents relating to the actions the committees took.

"Yes, and I will look for connections to scientists, engineers and manufacturing firms in any of the related technologies."

"I didn't get any sleep, last night, so I'm going home for some rest. You can reach me on my portable if we need to talk."

When Maritou returned to her office, later in the day, she could see that Lore Li had been busy. She had installed a link board covering the entire wall next to Maritou's desk. Lore Li was arranging photos of persons of interest next to their names. Strings were stretched, here and there, indicating the connections she had already uncovered or suspected.

Sauhn Lin and Ben Ru were on the board with strings stretching to all those connections provided by Sauhn Lin. More photos and several documents littered Maritou's desktop.

"I hope you don't mind, but there is more room for all of this, here in your office," Lore Li explained.

"Not at all. This is going to be great."

"You're looking a lot fresher," Lore Li noted, feeling more than a touch of envy.

Cole appeared at the doorway.

"We were able to arrange the meeting with the accountant," He announced. "Where shall we bring him?"

"Thank you, Cole. I'll see him in Lore Li's office. I'll be in there working while Lore Li works in here."

Taking the documents Lore Li had put together she went into the adjoining office, leaving the door open.

She thought of Vin. He occupied a special place in her inner world. How lovely it would be if he were her son.

Vin was a "Newborn". Although he was also a Gentar, he was not immortal. In fact, rarely would a Gentar, born after the trauma of the Vulan invasion of Hogar, become so.

He had been one of Maritou's students.

"Newborns," meaning those born after the launch of the Armada, were largely neglected. Maritou recognized this and joined ranks with a handful of others, men and women, from both species, who also saw the need and they formed a school.

Luckily for Vin, Maritou was one of those rare individuals capable of recognizing the gifts and talents of those who were commonly deemed slow, weird, socially inept or just plain stupid. By the time he met Maritou, he had bought into the idea that he was an incompetent buffoon. He had fashioned himself into a clown to shield himself from the scorn laid upon him by his peers, hiding his dyslexia behind his antics.

But Maritou, who was approaching her third millennium, was able to look through his outer shell and recognize his essence. He touched her deeply. It was like finding a wounded animal!

Waiting for him to arrive, she wondered how he had changed in the years since she had seen him.

She was immersed in the committee reports when she got the call announcing Vin's arrival.

"Yes, bring him over."

She checked in on Lore Li for a moment, closed the door between their offices, and opened the outer door to greet Vin.

"Number Two!" he shouted in delight.

Vin was the only other person, other than Venahus, who called her that.

She opened her arms and they embraced.

"It's good to see you, again, Vinnie! Let's sit over here."

She indicated some lounge chairs in the corner of the office.

"I didn't expect to see you here," he exclaimed.

"I know you didn't."

"So, where are the papers I need to sign?" he joked.

"Papers?"

"Yes, I was asked to go to the Recorder's Office, when I got off work, to sign some document that was misplaced. When I got to Recording, someone escorted me here."

"I see." Maritou chuckled.

She noted how much his personality had continued to open up since she had talked with him last.

"It must be something important?"

"Yes! Vital, in fact. I need your talents."

"Are you a secret agent, now? 'Number Two?'—Hmm?"

The way he said it made her laugh. "Well, let's say—temporarily."

'I'm intrigued. Who can I kill for you?"

"First, tell me how you've been, and bring me up to date. It's been too long." She didn't need to rush things. After this, she planned to go home and get a real night's sleep.

"Well, nobody has asked me how I am doing for some time," Vin said, "except of course, those who are just looking for a one syllable response."

Sadly, she noticed how much he had aged and was reminded of his mortality. She said nothing as she waited for him to gather his thoughts.

As he did, he realized how much he longed to share himself with someone truly interested.

"You know, I was angry over a lot of things, and for so long. I don't know what I would have done if you hadn't believed in me. By the time I graduated, I had dreams of becoming an auditor for one of the best firms."

"I remember," she encouraged.

"I was hired, but I've never been promoted. For a long time, I couldn't understand why. I didn't want to believe that my Vulan bosses are so prejudiced that they were holding me back because I'm a Gentar—and a Newborn. Holding me back on merit didn't make sense. The audit managers rely on me to produce. I do the work of an auditor, without the recognition. I came to realize that I've become more skilled than any of them."

"I believe that." Maritou agreed.

"I've come to the conclusion that most of them are not doing it consciously. Many appear to be my friends and I'm very sought after with each reassignment. It's comical to see them fight over me. They know my work will make them look good.

"It would be nice to have the title and the money," he continued, "but those things don't really matter that much. What does matter, is that I found out that my application to be recommissioned has been denied."

"No!" Maritou gasped.

As long as a crew member has their recommissioning, they will be reconstituted soon after death. Otherwise, under the Constitution, their memory crystals and DNA are stored for a time when they are needed for colonization of an alien planet. That is, except for Newborns, who have no protection under the Constitution. For them, death is probably the end.

She took Vin's hand and solemnly waited for him to continue.

"Dying wouldn't really be so bad if I hadn't made plans. I've saved enough to start my own firm in my—'second life' shall I say. Be my own man.

"Do you have anything to drink?" he asked. "Water?"

She went to the desk phone and dialed reception.

"Yes, what do we have here to drink?" . . . Okay.

Looking at Vin, "We have about anything you want."

"Some hot Moon Flower Tea?" he asked.

"Moon Flower Tea?" she asked the receptionist. "Good. Two of those, please, and some water."

To lighten the mood, Maritou started to reminisce about Vin's school days while they waited for the tea.

"Do you remember the math teacher, Mern de Kornah?" she asked.

"Yes. I don't think she ever liked me. I felt it the first day we met. I don't think she liked any of us Gentars.

"I think you are right."

"And she thought I was so stupid," said Vin. "I wanted her to like me, so I really worked hard and did well in her classes. But that didn't seem to impress her. So, I went to work, in secret, to solve that math problem she had been working on for years. When I came up with the answer, I showed her my equations."

"Was she impressed?"

"I don't know, really. She seemed to be getting sick and, suddenly, she left the classroom and didn't come back. I never saw her again."

"That must have been the day she resigned without an explanation," Maritou revealed.

"I've always suspected that she didn't like it that someone else solved her problem," Vin said. "Now I'm certain. I hope she eventually came to accept it and, somehow, was able to forgive."

The tea came and the pair drank slowly, welcoming the calming effect of the herbs. Finally, Maritou spoke. "As I told you Vin, I need your help with something."

"You name it."

"We suspect that someone has set up an unauthorized scientific research lab and, likely, some production facilities. We are dealing with some very clever and dangerous people here, Vin. They are probably terrorists. If you decide to take on this mission, your life would be in great danger should you be discovered.

"I'm in!" he affirmed.

"Okay, here is a list of supplies and equipment that I think would be needed to set up and operate the facilities we want to find."

Vin studied the list. "High tech stuff," he concluded. "How many areas of technology are involved, do you think?"

"A lot. Most likely, nanochips, entomology, genetics, object recognition software, wireless technologies, just to mention the most obvious."

"Follow the flow of materials and find the quarry, right?"

"You've got the picture. And, another thing—I think there is at least one person living in that research lab. She's a prisoner there, a Gentar."

"Oh?"

"Yes, she was kidnapped in Post Launch Year 1298. The lab was probably set up earlier and waiting for her.

"That narrows things down for me," Vin said. "I should have some results in the next few days."

"Good. But I can't say 'be careful' too many times. The terrorists have suffered a major setback and are probably regrouping. This makes them unpredictable and more dangerous."

"The best place for me to work on this will be in my own office, or a client's office," Vin remarked. "From there, I can have access to all of the archive files through my portable computer which goes with me everywhere I work."

Maritou handed him a pen. "Take this. It has a built-in transmitter. When you are ready to meet, again, push down hard on the point and it will send me a signal. Then, just wait where you are and someone will come and leave instructions on where to go. Do you have any questions?"

"No, I know what I need to do."

"Good luck, Vinnie!"

Maritou worked a while longer after Vin left. Her thoughts soon turned to Gar. She had been too exhausted, earlier in the day, to contribute much to their lovemaking and fell asleep while he took his pleasure. When she awoke, she promised him a proper encounter and they made a date for that evening.

Arriving at the apartment before him, she prepared a light dinner. She loved to cook for him and then watch him eat, savoring everything.

It wasn't long before he appeared, coming up behind her in the kitchen. His arms circled her supple waist and he kissed her tenderly under the ear.

"Smells good—the food, I mean."

"Here, try this," she said, as she turned and held her creation to his mouth.

"Yum! What is that?"

"They're toasted Williper leaves. A new friend of mine taught me how to make them."

"They're wonderful."

"How was the rest of your day?" she asked. "I understand that you went to see Arohn."

"He has asked me to take over command of the Armada, for now. So, I won't be able to work on the saucer for a while. Arohn will be commanding the reserve military which, ostensibly, has been called up for 'routine training'. As a reservist, you have been called, too, Arohn tells me."

"I'll be training a platoon of special operations forces that I may need in order to penetrate the conspirators' research lab, if it can be found. And, it's starting to look like we might see some action, soon. But enough of that. This is our night."

She went to him and he pulled her tight. She softly bit his lower lip before opening her mouth to receive his tongue. This was definitely turning into the "proper encounter" that she had promised.

"Can you reach the oven? Turn it off!" she ordered. "Dinner can wait."

Chapter 17

Game Plan

I like your investigation board," Maritou praised, as she walked into the office to find Lore Li hanging another connection.

"Thank you."

Maritou studied the board, giving close attention to the Dulamar Brothers and their key associates.

"Tell me more about Dulamar Materials. I see the company was formed not too long after Mihn's disappearance."

Lore Li thumbed through her notes.

"Let's see—The brothers formed the company when they purchased a defunct manufacturing facility and some equipment from MicroRobotics Solutions. MicroRobotics is an old company which continues to develop robotic technology for planet exploration and colonization. The brothers have no ownership interest in MicroRobotics and the only other connection I've found is that MicroRobotics buys some of its supplies from Dulamar Materials.

"Dulamar has two divisions," Lore Li continued, "a manufacturing division and another division that produces specialty chemicals and purified semiconductor materials for use in chip manufacturing."

"Interesting."

"It's the manufacturing division that is a mystery," Lore Li exclaimed. "They have a source of revenue that isn't reflected in their billing reports. Their financial statements show a lot more income than I can glean from their invoices. It looks as if they are doing some creative bookkeeping.

"And another interesting thing is that, while the controlling interest in Dulamar is held by the brothers, most of the capital was contributed by its minority shareholder, the Gentar tycoon, Nahmed Hosah. I've asked Cole to have his team track Hosah's movements around the time of his investment. They are piecing together old video recordings. Cole says it will take a while."

"Good work. Have you turned up anything on the ancient art of leaf folding? Mihn says that the helmets would be practically impossible to manufacture otherwise. The microprocessors the helmets are made from, are produced on incredibly thin flat sheets and then folded using a program that incorporates the principles of leaf folding."

"Yes, I did find out that that program was developed with the help of the Gentar sculptress, Mylas Eberhus who sometimes uses leaf folding in her artwork."

"Right. I knew Mylas back on Hogar before the Vulan invasion. She had been a frequent guest at the parties hosted by Gar and O'Ruhn. She is one of us Ancients. I'll go pay her a visit."

"Shall I get a message to Vin to alert him to Dulamar Materials?" Lore Li suggested.

"No, Vin will surely find that on his own. We would just be slowing him down."

"Didn't you say that he is dyslexic?" Lore Li said doubtfully.

"Yes, he is. But he learned to recognize his vulnerabilities, long ago, and how to compensate for them. Dyslexia is actually a positive factor in the performance of his area of genius. It just means that he is seeing so many more possibilities all at once than an ordinary individual has the capacity for. Those with dyslexia appear to be slow to the rest of the world, which tends to misunderstand and discourage them by shaming them in some way. Honoring them from infancy will produce brilliant minds. I think Vin will surprise you."

"I was hoping to see you, again!" Sauhn Lin greeted Maritou.

He wasn't restrained, this time, per her orders. His wings were still bandaged.

"How are you, Sauhn?"

"I'm okay."

"Good. Your stay here is indefinite. Eventually, I'm sure you will be transferred someplace better equipped where you can exercise and interact with other prisoners."

"I think I'm okay, for now. Thanks."

"I just came to see you to fill in a few gaps. Have you remembered anything you haven't told us, so far?"

He shook his head and she had no reason to think he was holding back anything deliberately.

"It appears that Ben Ru may have been involved with persons that you have not mentioned. What do you think about that? You know—you being his right-hand man. Do you think he had secrets from you?"

Sauhn thought about that and exclaimed, finally, "I really don't know what to think. It does surprise me. But I do see that he had plenty of opportunities because we did spend a significant amount of time apart. I do have my duties with maintaining the telescopes and tethers. Or, I did have," he corrected. "I guess I didn't know what Ben Ru did when I wasn't with him."

"Have you ever been to the Solay Mahn Array with him?"

"With Ben Ru? No. I think I was there just one time. I was called in to help inspect the tethers, which requires someone used to working in a space-suit. I was there several days, but Ben Ru had no reason to go. That was centuries ago."

"What if I told you that he's been going there frequently, over the past two hundred years?"

Sauhn shrugged and shook his head.

"Do you know the Dulamar brothers?" she asked.

"Mi Dulamar, the Councilman?"

"Yes."

"Well, I just know of him. I didn't know he had a brother."

Maritou also asked about Mihn Rova and Nahmed Hosah. He knew nothing of them.

It was beginning to look like there was an entirely separate network of conspirators, with Ben Rue appearing to be the only common link. She shivered to think that nothing was really known about their capabilities, their plans, or the extent of their network.

"Maritou?"

"Yes Sauhn?"

"I've had some time to think about things. And, I want you to know—I'm sorry for what I've done. Not only for what I tried to do to you, but for a lot of things."

She looked at him closely.

"I've come to realize that I'm not the great person that I thought myself to be," he continued. "You know—the smartest, fastest, strongest. I guess it doesn't matter what they do to me—how I am punished. I want to spend the time I have left, trying to do better."

"I've checked your work records, Sauhn. They're impressive. And that says something for you."

"I have enjoyed my work and I hope I can still be useful in some way."

"Thank you for your apology, Sauhn."

As she left the interrogation room, she turned.

His eyes reflected the bitter sweet admiration he felt for her. It had been the catalyst for his transformation.

"Good luck Sauhn!"

Mylas Eberhus was busy in her studio and didn't hear Maritou enter the gallery.

Maritou had always admired Mylas's work and was drawn to a large sculpture of two lovers in the middle of the showroom.

Across from the sculpture was a rather large painting—again of two lovers—Mylas and O'Ruhn.

"How stunningly erotic!" Maritou lauded.

Mylas appeared, coming out of her studio. "Why Maritou! I haven't seen you for a long, long time," she exclaimed, genuinely delighted to see her old friend, again. "How are you?"

"Good. Good. And you are looking great."

Mylas wore sandals and a short artist's apron covered with paints. Maritou guessed that she wore nothing underneath. The skin, on her gorgeous legs and arms, glowed like burnished bronze.

"In fact, you get more beautiful as time goes by," Maritou said.

"Look who's talking."

Maritou gestured to the many paintings in the gallery. "I see that you have taken up the brush. Are all of these your work?"

"Most of them."

"I love them. And I want one that will fit into our apartment. Would you do one of Gar and me?"

"Oh, yes! But the two of you will need to pose."

There was another sculpture that caught Maritou's eye, and she went to it. It was a giant leaf folding of an insect helmet. The single folded sheet, from which it was fashioned, was replete with oversized circuits and transistors.

"This is actually what I've come to talk to you about."

"It is one of the most complicated foldings I have ever done," Mylas explained. "I was asked to design one to fit a range of actual head sizes to fit Rovabots. Once I was finished, someone designed the circuitry which had to line up in all the right places for it to function."

"Have you been asked to design other helmets, similar to this?"

"Yes, but I told them that I will not do another. But they kept coming back. Finally, I agreed to train another artist to do it, but only one capable of understanding the art. I really thought this person would fail, but he surprised me."

"Who were the ones asking? And who did they send?"

"Well, the last one to make the request was a Vulan with a strange name that I don't remember. But the Gentar that they sent—I never will forget him. We spent as much time in my bed as we did in the studio. He was a good student, too. I wish he would come back sometime."

"What was his name?"

"It was Ben. Captain Ben Ru."

Maritou was stunned, but soon realized that it made sense.

"Did he ever talk about what he would do with his new skills?"

"Ah, no. I assumed he wanted to design helmets that would be manufactured on Solay Mahn. That is where the Vulan was from."

"How about his associates? Did he ever bring anyone else, or talk about others?"

"No, I would remember that."

"Mylas, you've given me more than I had hoped. Thank you! And, for now, please do not mention my visit to anyone. It would be dangerous. I'll come to visit, again, and tell you everything. Agreed?"

"Okay."

Chapter 18

Quick Study

Vin was in Maritou's office when she returned from her visit with Mylas. She introduced him to Lore Li. He had used the pen less than a day into his assignment.

"I've uncovered some peculiar facts," Vin explained.

"I have more work to do, but I thought you needed to know right away what I've learned so far. Anyway, I discovered a flurry of shipments of high-tech equipment and supplies that started in the year PL 1297. It was delivered to a warehouse in MC3 an asteroid of the MerCon Group."

"Let's see what data we have on the Mer Con Group," Maritou said, speaking to Lore Li.

Lore Li checked the data base.

"It indicates here that MerCon facilities are strictly warehouses." Lore Li reported. "Let's see—MC3 holds worn out drilling equipment, plasma engines and a large inventory of incubators. It's a large warehouse with 35% of its capacity available. It says nothing here about scientific equipment."

"I checked the personnel records," Vin added. "There's only one crewmember stationed there, permanently, a Vulan, name of Adil de NakshahOak."

"Do we know what is held in the other warehouses?" Maritou asked Lore Li.

"There are a lot of surplus items listed—materials to refit asteroids, such as tethering materials, more plasma engines, probes to explore candidate planets, and more incubators to reconstitute colonists when the time comes to inhabit a new world."

"Well, there is something strange occurring there," Vin exclaimed. "The only shipments recorded, after those initial deliveries of scientific equipment, are provisions for de NakshahOak and maintenance items for the MerCon asteroids.

"And this didn't make sense to me," Vin continued. "I suspected that someone was covering their tracks by falsifying the shipping records. But there are things they haven't been able to tamper with."

"Yes?" Maritou coaxed.

"Yes. From the early days of asteroid development, the radar tracking station, here on XK1, has recorded each flight ever made since the station commenced operations. It keeps track of the identity of each vessel, the exact times, points of origin and destinations, the pilots, and a lot of other data. It doesn't record the payloads, though, but I was able to determine those details from the accounting records."

Vin handed Maritou a memory pearl. "This is a list of all flights to and from MerCon over the relevant time period, and a detailed description of most of the payloads, and who the crew members were. However, the records available to me do not provide a way to determine who any of the passengers were on any of the personnel shuttles."

"We can determine that from the video archives," Lore Li offered.

"Good work, Vin," Maritou praised. "What else will I learn from the memory pearl?"

"That is an enigma!" Vin declared. "You'll see that for many years, the actual shipments were consistent with your belief about a high-tech lab with a limited number of researchers. You can tell from the dietary provisions that this included both Gentars and Vulans. Then, you will see a recent change."

Vin reached for the memory pearl. "May I?"

He loaded the pearl in Lore Li's computer.

"Look at this," he pointed out on the screen. "Starting here, look at the boost in provisions for Vulan personnel. And this has continued to increase. There is enough fungus going in there to feed dozens. And, the scary thing is that the shipments are starting to include assault weapons, ostensibly for storage."

Maritou and Lore Li looked at each other, dumbstruck.

"I have an idea," Lore Li exclaimed. "We can take a census of the entire Armada. It has been a while since one has been done. We can pass it off as routine. Then, we should be able to deduce who is actually in there."

"Excellent," Maritou agreed. "And let's get some help from Cole's team. It's going to be time consuming to develop passenger lists for these flights to MerCon. What do you think, Vin?"

"It shouldn't take long because there are relatively few flights over the time period in question. I suggest assembling a small team of four or five and having them start with the personnel shuttles and supply ships carrying unusual cargo. I've also started another list of flights between all the other points common to MerCon. This would be a massive list if I included every flight. So, I am concentrating on samples from interesting time periods.

"I can work with that," Lore Li declared. "You are really something, Vin."

"Thank you."

"Let's get started on this," Maritou urged, approving the plan.

"Yes," Vin said, "but there is more. My investigation revealed another coverup. One of the companies involved is the maker of the predator helmets used by Mihn Rova's pest killers. Another company claims to be the manufacturer, but actually manufactures nothing. It's just a shell."

Maritou had a hunch but kept it to herself. She wanted to hear it from Vin.

"And the names of these companies? she asked.

"The actual product is produced by Dulamar Manufacturing which sells it, indirectly, using the shell company, Kofi Products."

"And who owns Kofi Products?"

"It's wholly owned by the wife of Nahmed Hosah," Vin said.

Maritou and Lore Li exchanged knowing smiles.

"Please, let me in on the joke," Vin asked.

Lore Li laughed, mildly. "Well, we discovered, ourselves, that something was out of order with Dulamar and I suggested we alert you to it. But Maritou assured me that it was better to see what you turned up on your own. She was right."

"Vin?" Maritou asked. "I have something to ask you, but I want you to consider it carefully before you decide."

"Okay."

"You have taken on a key role in our entire operation, here. It's a risky assignment but up until now, I don't think what you are doing has aroused suspicion. But that may change if you continue."

"I told you, Maritou, I'm in all the way."

"As long as you understand the risk, I will ask you if you want to come on full-time and work here, in the office, with us. Cole says he can always use someone with your talents."

"Ah! This means I'm a spy, too. And, since I've only had one life, you can start calling me Number One. Right Number Two?"

"Seriously!" Maritou pretended to scold. "Now, let's get to work."

Chapter 19

It's Not Too Late!

O'Ruhn was in a rage. Sten's trail had run cold. O'Ruhn, after examining the video clip of his son's escape, was convinced that he was in league with le Noir and his forces.

"Sten's a weakling! I've always tried to mold him into the kind of son that would make any father proud," O'Ruhn told Zelena through clenched teeth. "When I get my hands on him—"

"Why wait?" she cooed.

"What do you mean?"

"Anya, Sten's fiancée is here." Zelena sang.

Zelena was one of O'Ruhn's minions, the scheming one. Her sexual appetites were best satisfied when she would take part in a ceremony where O'Ruhn sacrificed a young Abaru. Especially, if one of the victim's loved ones was there to witness the carnage.

"Oh, don't think that I have forgotten Anya! I'm saving her for when my son is captured. He can enjoy the spectacle from the audience."

Aroused with this image in her mind, she exhalted, "And I can entertain him while he watches you remove her head!"

"Don't worry, you'll have your fun," he told her.

Drawn to his own fantasy he snarled, revealing the twelve front teeth sharpened for flesh tearing efficiency.

"Now, go get the others and have them meet us in the party room. And while you are at it, have someone send Anya to the fattening room. She is too skinny for my taste."

"You know, there is a fresh shipment of Abarus—let's really have a party." she begged.

"Tomorrow! I haven't inspected them, yet."

O'Ruhn came away from the party room unsatisfied and feeling powerless. Lately, it seemed, things were getting out of hand. First, the military failed to get past Arohn's stronghold on Vul. Then, he had lost control of the government which had awarded the Vespi contract to Rayloh. And then, Rayloh disappeared before he could be assassinated. And now, his son's betrayal.

BarOak was waiting for O'Ruhn to discuss the latest developments in the search for Sten.

"We have not found Maritou. She hasn't been seen since Rayloh disappeared."

"You know, Arohn is behind all of this," O'Ruhn hissed.

"We don't know, for sure. But we must be prepared," BarOak said.

"What could they be planning? Where are we the most vulnerable?"

"I think the question is, where are they the most vulnerable. Arohn le Noir knows we will not give up on penetrating his defenses on Vul. We will either find a way to get inside his lava tubes, or we will send Krell, or another large asteroid to destroy the whole planet. But if I were le Noir, I would focus on the more immediate threat of having his shield destroyed by a nuclear device."

"To do that," O'Ruhn protested, "we would have to figure out how he is preventing our bombs from detonating."

"We are working on that, and we might find a breakthrough. But even that will take time. We believe that he has created some type of force field which interferes with the nuclear reaction. He must be using subatomic particles, and we are far behind him in that technology. The good news is, he doesn't know that."

"So, if you were le Noir, you would try to prevent the short-term threat."

"Yes, and since his spaceships are superior to ours, that would be my plan—to destroy our fleet. Even though we have him outnumbered, he can surely outmaneuver our ships in open space. For now, we are vulnerable and he knows that. My biggest fear is that, if his force field can prevent our warheads from detonating, perhaps he can do something to detonate them in the launch tubes of our ships. I think we had better relocate our fleet, for now."

"Do it. And then figure out a way to destroy him," O'Ruhn ordered, impotently.

"Yes," BarOak answered.

BarOak had no idea how to get to le Noir but knew it was best not to stir O'Ruhn's frustration, lest it boil over on himself.

"There is something else," BarOak announced.

He handed O'Ruhn a message that had taken some one hundred and fifty years to arrive.

"Here is the latest from Ben Ru."

Greetings,

Everything here on-track. Progress on the insect project is promising and we should have a prototype, soon. Work on the replication technology is coming along and we have access to plenty of incubators. Observations indicate that Solar System W-292 may become our best target for colonization. We will know more after Fixed Infrared Telescope "Mega" is one-line. Per your orders, once we are certain that W-292 is our choice, and we have the replication technology, your reproduction will commence.

Your servant, Col. Ben Ru

O'Ruhn dismissed BarOak. He wanted to be alone with his dark thoughts.

He reread Ben Ru's message and felt uneasy. Before the Armada launched, he had managed to have two of his memory crystals smuggled aboard in Ben Ru's safe-keeping.

His original orders were to have him reproduced with his earliest memory crystal. He had never reversed that order and, now it was probably too late. Before countermanding orders could reach Ben Ru, His duplicate would likely be in place.

One more load to carry! Confound you, Maritou!

He tried to think of ways he would do her violence when he got his hands on her. But, instead, he found himself wanting to be held and soothed by her as she softly reminded him, "It's not too late."

Chapter 20

The Swarm

Vin hopped the late shuttle from XK1 to his apartment in a nearby residential array. He anticipated the sensation of sliding into the cool and smooth bedding that would warm him as he surrendered his thoughts in slumber.

There were no other passengers on the shuttle and he turned off the cabin lights, closed his eyes, and allowed his whole body to go limp and release his tensions to the weightlessness of space.

He reflected on his experiences of the last few days—seeing Maritou again and the challenge and excitement of the secret work he was doing. It was really quite refreshing.

How different Maritou was from the parents who had neglected him and had left him mostly alone to navigate his own childhood and the subculture of the Newborns.

He had one more chance to apply for reconsideration for being reconstituted.

If things go well with my efforts to help Maritou, the recognition I will receive for this contribution might be enough to win the approval of the Renewal Board.

His spirits were high as he made his way from the shuttle port to his apartment.

Reaching for the door, his assailants were on him without warning. They went for the neck with deadly aim.

He remained conscious long enough to realize that death was imminent and to taste the failure of his bid for renewal.

Cole's call pulled Maritou from the early stages of sleep. He explained to her what the security cameras had recorded.

"Our agents reached him a few moments ago. He's dead!" Cole choked.

"No! This can't be happening!" Maritou snapped; her disbelief quickly turning to anger.

Gar, not knowing what was being discussed, joined her at the edge of the bed, soothing her with one hand.

Cole sent her the footage from the attack and she and Gar watched it together on her portable.

The video showed Vin reaching to open his door. Suddenly, his head jerked to one side and he slapped his neck. His whole body jerked spasmodically as his hands brushed wildly under his ears. Dropping to one knee, he struggled to stand, and fell forward to the palms of his hands and then to the floor. The spasms slowly subsided and he lay motionless with one hand outstretched as if reaching for the door.

Stunned, Maritou sat, observing the wild feelings that surged through her body. Thoughts and images raced across her mind. She knew she had to find a place, within, where she could regain her footing. With great effort, she pulled herself away from the darkness that loomed ahead. For now, she had to be cold!

"Tell the agents not to move him and to arrest anyone who tries to leave the asteroid. I'm going there now. Have a forensic team meet me." Maritou instructed.

"Let's go together," Cole told her. "We'll meet you at the shuttle port."

"And Cole, have them equipped with hazardous material suits and bring enough for you, me, and the other agents."

Solemnly, Maritou and Cole waited for the shuttle door to open as Cole began to explain, "His body guards did everything by the book."

The door opened and they filed in with Cole's team.

"I know they did, Cole. If I blame anyone, I blame myself first. We're not up against a conventional enemy."

"It looked as if Vin had been attacked by something crawling on him. What could you have done?" Cole protested.

"Once I met with Mihn Rova, I could have acted right away and anticipated something like this."

"No! You did your part by sounding the alarm when you briefed us upon your return from your meeting with Mihn. It's only been two days. Arohn is already taking action on this, he tells me. It's in his hands."

Maritou turned on the intercom in the shuttle and gave instruction to the forensic team. "It's likely that the victim was attacked by poisonous insects." she began.

She paused, struggling to distance her thoughts and the words she was forming, from the anger and grief that burned in her breast.

"Approach the body slowly, methodically, searching for tiny objects and insects. Once the surrounding area is cleared, search the body and clothing. Then the medical examiners can begin their work."

When the team reached the hallway to Vin's apartment, Maritou held back and let Cole and the others proceed. She needed to stay objective and felt it best to avoid the sight of Vinnie in death. Sucking up as much saliva as she could, she swallowed hard, trying to wet the dry lump in her throat.

She checked the time. It was early, but she needed help and pulled out her portable.

"Lore Li?"

"Yes," Lore Li responded. "Has something happened?"

"It has. Something terrible. Vin has been killed!"

"Vin? No!" Lore Li cried.

"It looks as if he was attacked by insects as he reached his apartment last night. If you can go to the office, I'd like you to check all of the video recordings in his asteroid before and after the attack. Get back to me with anything unusual."

"Will do. And Maritou? I know Vin meant a lot to you. I'm sorry!"

"Thank you."

Maritou dialed Arohn. He was the Commander-in-Chief of the military and, when he answered, he told her he had just been briefed by Cole. He was on his way as soon as he could muster some troops.

"Unless the attack was carried out remotely," she told Arohn, "the attackers are trapped here. I have Lore Li checking the camera recordings. Do you have any gear to defend a possible insect attack? All we have are hazmat suits, and they are cumbersome."

"We have taken counter measures," he assured her. "I'll explain when we get there."

Maritou was on the phone with Lore Li when Arohn arrived. Lore Li was not finished working through the recordings but had discovered the probable avenue of attack. Earlier, the day of the attack, a two-man maintenance crew was recorded removing a ventilation duct cover in the level above Vin's apartment. Their cart blocked a complete view of the duct, but it appeared that they placed something inside before replacing the cover.

"I tracked the movements of this pair before and after the attack," Lore Li continued. "They came and left the asteroid through the supply port. So I tracked their flights in and out-bound. Their utility ship is registered to a company that doesn't exist. The point of departure and point of return being the same—The Indersol Supply and Maintenance Group.

" Good work! Keep following your instincts."

Arohn wore a protective hood with a wrap-around visor of fine screen. His clothing was fully covered with a mesh fabric overall. He was alone when he walked up to Maritou.

"Where are your men?" she asked.

"They're covering the entrances. Come up with me to the utility port and I'll show you what we've been working on."

As they made their way up to the maintenance section of the asteroid, she commented on his gear. "I like your suit. It looks simple and effective."

"It's comfortable, too. We are working on prototypes that can be worn with full battle gear. The design for Gentars has more problems because of the wings," he told her.

"We can't fight as well without our wings," she said resolutely.

Arohn took her to the supply port. She estimated that there were about a dozen men in the receiving area of the port. They were using it as a staging area.

Arohn introduced her to a Vulan officer bringing in several odd-looking containers. "Maritou, this is Lieutenant du Mantahn."

"Nice to meet you, Ma'am!"

"My pleasure. Just call me Maritou."

There was a faint hum emanating from the containers.

"Those are swarming vessels, aren't they?" She asked.

"Yes, they are," du Mantahn agreed proudly.

"Give Maritou a demonstration of what your Rova Defenders can do," Arohn ordered.

Du Mantahn handed a wristband to Arohn, who put it on.

"The Defenders can be instructed to protect anyone wearing a specific wristband."

He removed one of the swarming vessels and took out a controller he carried in a holster.

"This controller will send instructions to the swarm inside the vessel," the lieutenant said as he pushed a series of buttons. "I'm just starting to discover all of the capabilities of these bots. Whoever designed this system is a true genius."

He opened the vessel and the swarm flew out and hovered gently above Arohn's head.

"They will attack any insect that comes close. Anyone within three paces of the wristband is also protected."

Maritou was always amused when anyone used "paces" to signify distances.

"You mean like this?" she said as she measured out three strides.

"No, like this," the lieutenant replied earnestly, as he stepped and counted.

"Lieutenant du Mantahn is one of my reserve officers," Arohn explained. "He's a grower in his civilian life and has centuries of experience with Rovabots."

Du Mantahn entered another command into the controller and the swarm flew back into their container.

"We call them Defender Bots, but they are simply the same Rovabots that are used by all growers," Arohn told her.

"As are the controllers. The only difference is the program used, du Mantahn added. "This is my personal controller that I use every day."

"Thank you for the demonstration, Lieutenant," Arohn told him. "Please assign a wristband to Maritou and I will keep this one."

"Yes sir!"

Du Mantahn showed Maritou a call button on the wristband.

"Hold this button down until you feel a vibration. It sends a command to a swarming vessel which will dispatch a swarm to protect you."

"Thank you, Lieutenant," she said.

Arohn gave orders to his men and three of them left to defend the forensic team.

"Okay, we're ready," he told Maritou. "Let's decide how to proceed. The residents here will be waking up soon and going off to work. Any news from Lore Li?"

"Yes, she spotted a maintenance crew doing something with the ventilation ducts in the level above Vin's apartment. As they were leaving, they passed through a blind spot and an inordinate amount of time passed before they emerged again. They must have stopped at one of the two apartments that are out of view from the cameras. I have two of Cole's agents covering that hallway. Lore Li will be sending us a list of all the residents and combinations to their doors."

"Maybe she has already sent it," Maritou said, checking her portable. "Yes, here it is." She forwarded a copy to Arohn and Cole and read aloud the attached message from Lore Li:

Maritou, this file includes photos of the residents. The video recordings show the residents of B110 and B111 arriving home, last night, before the attack on Vin. I await your orders.

In the meantime, I am gathering intel on the recent activity at the Solay Mahn Array.

"I like the way that girl operates," Maritou exclaimed.

"I like everything about her!" Arohn vaunted unexpectedly.

"I wondered about that. You hide it pretty well. You're going to tell me everything, later."

"Right! Now what do you say we pay a couple of visits?"

He pulled out his portable and ordered a detachment to meet them on Level B.

"No one has left the asteroid since the attack," Maritou said. "Assuming Vin was attacked by insects, the swarm must still be here in the asteroid, someplace.

"We won't leave here before we find it."

The detachment was sweeping the hallway for listening devices when Maritou and Arohn arrived on Level B. The squad leader had the ventilation duct open and his head inside. "There is something in here, sir."

"Let me have a look," Arohn said, as he poked his head in. "Looks like some type of radio device. Leave it in place and Col. BeCholn will take care of it."

"Okay, let's each take an apartment and go in at the same time," Arohn told Maritou. "You take B111."

He nodded to his bot keepers, and moments later swarms of Defender Bots were hovering around him and Maritou.

Maritou entered the apartment right behind two of her men, who held their weapons on a very frightened Vulan in business attire.

"Don't be alarmed, sir." Maritou advised him, as he was frisked for weapons. "If you have done nothing wrong, you have nothing to be concerned about."

"But what is this about? I need to leave for an appointment."

He looked very different from the photo of the Gentar woman that supposedly resided in this unit. Maritou motioned to the inner rooms of the apartment and the two solders went to search the bedroom.

"Why don't we sit down and talk a bit. Then you can go off to work."

Panic had set in. "No! I—ah—don't have time!"

Maritou kept toying with him because she sensed that, the more frightened he became, the more information he would give away once she hit him with the tough questions.

"What's in the case?" she asked, indicating the carrying case by the door.

"Nothing! Ah, just some merchandise samples."

"What's your name, sir?"

"Ah—"

He was not prepared to give a false name and his panic increased as he desperately tried to invent one. In desperation, he gave the name of a childhood friend.

She checked her watch and decided to stop wasting time. Her tone remained friendly. "I'll tell you what's going to happen, now. We're going to have a peek inside your case, and then you are going to tell me your real name."

"But you don't understand! They made me help them."

"I see," she said.

The soldiers reappeared from the back rooms with the apartment's legitimate resident, looking angry and confused but unharmed.

"This person will not bother you again," Maritou reassured the Gentar woman. "I'm sorry for your ordeal. Please go with this soldier now, and everything will be explained to you."

Once the woman was gone, Maritou contacted Lore Li and adjusted her phone so Lore Li could hear everything.

"Lore Li, please verify the information that you are about to hear."

Maritou picked up the case and placed it on the dining table. She checked the time. It was not too late, but she had to move things along. Turning to her captive, her tone went from friendly to assertive.

"Okay, now just answer my questions as concisely as you can. We don't have much time and, believe me, it's in your best interest to cooperate. Understood?"

He nodded sheepishly.

"Is it safe for me to open this case?"

"Yes, but."

"Concise, remember?"

"Yes, it's okay."

She opened the lid and found what she was expecting.

"Where were you planning to go with this when you left here?"

"Back home. I live at the Regan Group."

"That's an agricultural array. I'm guessing you are a grower?"

He nodded.

"What's your real name?"

"What are you going to do with me?" he pleaded.

"Just answer my questions and your cooperation will weigh in your favor."

She pointed to her watch.

"Time is running out! Now, who are you?"

"Okay, my name is Irrod du Ouht. I'm just a grower. None of this was my idea!"

"And, whose idea was it?"

"I don't know, really. I get orders from a Vulan. Calls himself Duf. He says his boss will have us killed—my wife and me if I mess up."

Maritou spoke with one of the soldiers. "Have one of the bot keepers come in here and bring an empty vessel."

Lore Li interrupted.

"I ran the name Irrod du Ouht and the information checks out. I'm sending you his photo now."

"Thank you, Lore Li. Stay on the line."

"Now, Irrod," Maritou asked, as she checked his photo, "you were planning to catch the first shuttle out, this morning?"

"Yes."

Lieutenant du Mantahn, himself, appeared.

"Lieutenant, please remove a sample of this swarm," Maritou instructed. "Say, five of them. And keep them alive."

"Yes ma'am!"

"Okay, Irrod! You're going to catch that shuttle just like you were ordered to do. You're going to go back to your normal routine. You will advertise for a swarm handler to help you with the Rovabots you use in your growing operations and you will hire the one that gives

Du Mantahn Produce as a reference. This will be one of my agents. Do you understand me?"

"Yes—I guess so," he said, stunned at this change in fortune.

"You have aided in murder, here."

"But!"

"Just listen! You're working for us now. You will keep my agent informed of any communications with Duf."

She stepped briefly into the hallway and spoke with Arohn who ordered his troops to stand down. The morning commute would take place, as usual.

"Now, go!" she ordered du Ouht.

Chapter 21

Time Capsule

Fifteen Centuries Earlier

O'Ruhn and BarOak had amassed great wealth and power which continued to grow, despite their having become fugitives from Vulan justice. Their alliance forged a dynamic cartel—O'Ruhn and his lieutenants with BarOak, the brilliant scientist. Forced to stronghold in the depths of the Hogarian atmosphere, they waited for the departure of the Armada and the day they could rule the planet.

From the safety of their realm, they observed the new partnership of the Vulan and Gentar races as they prepared their asteroid fleet for its daring mission. By rights, they felt cheated as it surely should have been their mission.

Obsession is not hard to find amongst all thinking creatures. Obsession is distinct from compulsion. Desire is the foundation of obsession while the underpinnings of compulsion are varied and elusive. Obsession blinds the afflicted to better possibilities while endowing many with a sense of entitlement and sometimes spurs them towards unspeakable acts. And O'Ruhn was afflicted with the whole package.

At this point, O'Ruhn was in crisis. He could still save himself, he knew. But, to do so, he would have to give up his place and enter a world that threatened his very existence. And from the top of his ramparts, the fall would be unimaginable. And, he could never have Rena! And, what choices would he have?

Oftentimes, when pondering his dilemma, the embodiment of Maritou would take form. And her appearances, as real as they seemed, were hallucinatory, he was certain. But they were bewildering. *Why not Rena? I want Rena*, he would lament.

He didn't desire Maritou. So why in their short relationship had she left such a mark?

On this day, his thoughts were cut short by a call from BarOak who had news regarding his progress toward developing the reproduction technology that he had stolen from his great foe, Arohn de Vul, and from the actual creators, Rena and Gar.

"The memory crystallizer is ready," BarOak informed O'Ruhn.

"Really? Ready for me?"

"Yes." BarOak assured him, aware of O'Ruhn's trepidation. "Whenever you want to try it."

"But we have no incubators."

"No, not yet," BarOak admitted. "But it's just a matter of time. Meanwhile, you can record your memories whenever you want. One day you will be reproduced with a new body to encase your memories, from any of the crystals you choose."

"Let me think about it."

That night, exhausted and unable to sleep, O'Ruhn kept replaying that day's meeting with BarOak. *The idea of crystallization opens up more and more choices to agonize over. What are my choices?*

I can face justice for treason and slave trading. And I have no defense. I'm guilty and will be executed.

I can run and go back to the simple life of a hunter. Before the Vulan invasion and, before I met Rena, I lived contentedly. Maybe I could again.

Or I can be reproduced.

Until the Vulans brought their technologies and industrial might, the Gentar were hunter gatherers and traders. O'Ruhn and Gar lived in their camp at the edge of Mon Mari for centuries, ever since they were boyhood friends. Gar traded in his medicinal formulations and the unique gadgets he would invent. O'Ruhn was a hunter and widely sought after for the fine weapons his father taught him to make.

Yes, I could escape back to the old ways. There are still plenty of untamed islands where I can hunt and hide away.

He imagined himself flying through the cool air of the Hogarian heights, everything he owned and needed tied to his breast and strapped to his hips. And there would always be a pristine island ahead, full of game and ripe with lovely women.

But he could not hold on to this dream. It confronted him with the disquietude of knowing that something inside him was changing. On this night, he thought back to the day he had noticed it in the mirror. His skin seemed to be losing its radiance. And he began to heed the strange feelings of exhaustion, so foreign to him. He was aging; losing his immortality.

BarOak had noticed it, too, and had an idea. To survive the alien environment of Hogar, Vulans needed something in their diets—either immortal flesh, or "Life Blood," the fungus Rena had developed in Arohn's research lab. He encouraged O'Ruhn to partake. Maybe it would work for Gentars, too.

O'Ruhn had purchased his freedom from his Vulan captors by providing them with the Abaru victims that he was uniquely capable of snatching from their low-lying islands. But, up until now, he had never before tasted their flesh. The smell of it disgusted him, as did BarOak's suggestion, which threw him in a rage. In desperation, he finally agreed to sample "Life Blood" as long as it was placed in capsules so he didn't have to smell it.

The effect was almost immediate. Within a few days, he felt much stronger and his energy returned. Enthralled by the improvement, he found himself checking his image several times a day. What others noticed was the emergence of a more aggressive personality and an explosive temper.

Soon, he skipped the capsules and developed a liking for the raw fungus. And it wasn't long before the sight of bare Abaru flesh became irresistible.

This was the state he found himself in as he pondered his future. "Life Blood" would no longer be available to him if he ran. Dealing in slaves was one thing—but outright savagery?

So, I really have few options. He lamented.

But why would I even consider giving up my current position? The Armada will be leaving one day, and BarOak and I can come out of hiding and take power. Even now, the tendrils of our influence are tightening around the framework of what the Armada will leave behind.

O'Ruhn woke with a start, not realizing where he was. A soft hand caressed the side of his face. Maritou was sitting beside him on the bed! "It's not too late," she whispered—another hallucination but it seemed all too real.

At that moment, he made his decision.

"Okay, I'm ready," he told BarOak the next day. "Let's make two crystals. One of them will be on the Armada when it ventures away from the solar system."

"That shouldn't be difficult," BarOak noted. "Several of our lieutenants have already been cleared to serve as crewmen, including Sy Morah who, with his new name of Ben Ru, has been promoted to colonel and will head their main observatories."

"Speaking of Sy," O'Ruhn declared, "I've decided he should be our General. He should be given my crystal."

Chapter 22

... through a glass, darkly...

Present Time

Cole and his team had completed their work and moved themselves and Vin's body into the empty apartment before the early morning rush. They had almost given up on finding any insects at the crime scene when a dead one was discovered, helmet intact, in a fold of skin under one of Vin's wings. That and several blood samples constituted the sum total of the evidence that was added to the trove collected by Maritou.

Later, when Maritou, Cole and his team reached the office, there was a message from Gar waiting for Maritou.

She and Cole briefed each other on their findings and then she returned Gar's call.

Gar was now acting Commander of the fleet. He had received some disturbing news and wanted to call a meeting with her, Arohn and Cole as soon as possible.

She went straight to Cole's office when she ended the call with Gar.

"I was just about to come to you," Cole said. "While we were out, a message came through from our agents on the Centex Group."

"That must be what Gar wants to meet with us about," Maritou exclaimed. "He'd like to meet at the Command Center. When can you get away?"

"We can go now."

"I'll let Gar know."

"Arohn will be joining us in a few moments," Gar told them when they arrived.

Gar kissed Maritou. "You must be very tired," he told her. "You know, that cot is still there in your old office. Maybe you can rest awhile when we are done here."

Having spent yet another night with no sleep, Maritou didn't argue. "That's not a bad idea. I'm sure I'll be more effective if I do."

Cole had rarely been around Gar and Maritou, together. He wondered if they were always so loving and respectful with each other. They reminded him of the way he felt when he thought of Mihn Rova.

"What has happened?" Arohn asked, the moment he walked in.

"There's news from Centex," Gar said. "Cole, would you fill us in?"

"Sure. As we all know, for many years, now, the Mission has been gathering data on Solar System W-292. Most of the evidence has been provided by the Main Telescope Observatory on Centex, with its lineup of stationary telescopes. And Ben Ru has been in charge of this all along."

"Yes, and W-292 has become the Mission's number one candidate for colonization based on Ben Ru's data," Gar added.

"Well, it appears that the evidence has been doctored," Cole told them. "What we now believe to be the bona fide evidence was found, today, in a small office hidden at the back of a supply room. It was on Centex, close to Ben Ru's private quarters."

"How does this evidence differ from the tampered observations?" Maritou asked.

"That needs to be determined from careful analysis by whatever trusted astronomers that we can recruit," said Gar. "Unfortunately, most of our astronomers are on Sauhn Lin's list of conspirators."

"Venahus might be able to help," Maritou suggested. "Planetary science has become her area of expertise."

"We should contact her," Arohn asserted, with a concurring nod from Gar.

"Well, you should all know that orders came down early this morning from the Council," Gar revealed. "They have suddenly committed to W-292 and have ordered a course correction and for the deceleration sequence to begin in three days. They have commissioned a team of physicists to calculate a trajectory that will put us in an orbit around the inner planets.

"And it's more than peculiar," Gar continued. "We've already made calculations for the optimal trajectory plans. The farther we deviate from those plans, the more risk of not being able to take corrective action in the event of system failure with any one of our propulsion systems. I think someone wants us to be committed to W-292 before anyone gets wise to the deception."

"We'll just have to gather as much evidence as we can to cast doubt upon the advisability of altering our trajectory prematurely," Arohn suggested. "To be fair, W-292 may turn out to be an excellent choice."

"Would it be fatal to start the deceleration sequence and then accelerate, later?" Cole wondered.

"From an engineering perspective, no," Gar conceded. "I'm thinking more about the effect it would likely have on morale. Once the crew thinks we are headed to W-292, they will start dreaming. There will be a level of excitement not witnessed since the launch of our Mission. If we throw a wet blanket on it, who knows what may erupt?"

"This is starting to look like a mutiny." Arohn exclaimed. "Let's remind ourselves of something that Sauhn Lin told Maritou. He said that the conspirators' goal is to take over the mission."

Arohn hesitated.

"Yes?" Gar encouraged.

"Well, there is one issue that has been controversial since our other mutiny," Arohn said.

"Yes." Maritou interjected. "The mutineers wanted to colonize a solar system that had intelligent life on the two habitable planets. This went against the morals and ethics that we supposedly believe in, collectively, as colonizers. Since then, a growing number are questioning our official stance, which is written in our Constitution."

"Perhaps the mutineers would have prevailed had they not been so radical and violent," Gar suggested. "Our general population will not see the current chain of events as radical, unless they know they've been duped. And that makes our adversaries especially powerful."

"When does Council plan to announce their decision?" Arohn wondered.

"Tomorrow!" Gar replied.

"If I can find her, in time," Arohn said, "I will go talk to Councilwoman Uma de Corsa, an old friend of mine. Maybe she can influence the rest of the Council. What are your thoughts?"

"It might buy us a little time." Cole conceded.

"What about taking a slightly different approach?" Maritou said. "I think the conspirators want us to step into a trap and end up looking like the bad guys. We must admit that someone, maybe Ben Ru, has been a lot smarter than us for a long time."

"What do you propose?" Arohn asked.

"When you talk to the Councilwoman you could suggest that the two of you disclose the data discrepancy in a special session of the entire Council. Put the problem in their laps. Maybe it would be wise to have some faith in the legislative process. I have a feeling that there are plenty of Council members that will demand a reasonable delay in the decision to change our trajectory at this time."

"Yes," Gar reflected, "this would put our adversaries in a ticklish spot."

Arohn looked around for approval of Maritou's plan. "It appears that we have a consensus. Cole?"

"I need to stick with my spy work," said Cole. "I'm just thankful that my Commanders aren't a bunch of idiots. Go for it!"

"Okay," Arohn pronounced, "I think we all know our assignments. Let's get to work. That leaves you, Gar, to find out what the conspirators are attempting to hide with the falsified W-292 evidence."

Maritou left the meeting with Cole. "I do think I'll stop here for a while and see if that cot has gotten any softer. You have been up all night, too."

"I have a quiet spot of my own," he admitted.

"Do me a favor?" she asked. "Please get word to Mihn that I will be invading her apartment again tonight. Let her know that I'm bringing the food."

"I will. And, when you see her, would you deliver something for me?"

"Of course."

Chapter 23

W-292

Back on Hogar, the situation was unfolding rapidly. There had not yet been an opportunity to inform anyone on the Armada that Rayloh and Naomi had received the memories of Gar and Rena and that they were both adjusting well. It would take time, of course, for them to integrate their new and expanded identities. Their basic personalities were largely unchanged, although there were definitely some challenges in accepting new points of view.

Rayloh and Naomi joined Sten for the daily combat training with Maritou Venahus and this was their second day. Maritou started by running the class through their morning flight exercises and then started in on evasive maneuver drills.

"This next move will feel perfectly unnatural at first," she told her class. "You will be moving your wings in a whole new way. Let me demonstrate. This is one of the most effective moves to counter a frontal attack."

She nodded to one of the training assistants and he lunged at her with a knife. Her movements were too much of a blur for anyone to track with their eyes. All at once, her body pivoted ninety degrees and shot backwards, away from the path of the blade. Her open hand, carried by the momentum of her spin, found its mark on the backside of the assailant's wrist. The knife flew harmlessly to one side. Her wings moved again, and she left the ground, twisting in the opposite direction as she launched her kick, which may have proved deadly had she not pulled it up short of her attacker's neck. The entire thing was captured on a video camera.

Rayloh and Sten were convinced they were incapable of such a feat. But with Rena's memories, Naomi already knew the technique. She just needed practice, and to get her body in shape.

"Now, I realize that that all took place faster than you could follow," Maritou said. "So, let's break it down into pieces. Today, we'll work on the initial spin and the backward movement. Watch this in slow-motion."

She cued the assistant who ran close up footage of Maritou's actions.

"Now, start by following the basic wing movements."

She worked with each of them, patiently, until they gained a bit of confidence and comfort with this new challenge.

Arohn le Noir appeared.

"Gar is on the radio. He wants to talk to us. Says it's urgent."

"Okay, get some refreshments," she told her students. "And then practice the stuff that we worked on yesterday. I'll be back."

"We have a situation here." Gar began.

He briefed Maritou and le Noir on the W-292 implications and the political pressure to alter their trajectory.

"We believe our best course is to prove Ben Ru's data false and expose it as an attempt to mislead Council and get them to commit the Mission to W-292."

"And you need an astronomer to help you," le Noir surmised.

"Exactly!" Gar agreed. "The best astronomers we have here are Ben Ru's people. And they are all under suspicion. We need Maritou."

"What types of differences have been noticed?" Maritou asked, coming directly to the point.

"There are anomalies in the visible light images," Gar noted. "Our concern is that this may indicate the possibility of intelligent life on the W-292 habitable planets.

"And what about the search for radio signals?" Venahus wondered.

"Nothing was found that conflicts with the official studies. If there is intelligent life on W-292, it isn't communicating via analog radio signals. Those would have been detected."

"So if there are civilizations on those planets, their technologies have either not advanced far enough to have discovered radio waves or have advanced beyond the need for them. They could be listening to us chatter right now," she ventured. "I'll have a look at the images and get back to you. It will have to be quick because we are in training for the rescue mission."

"Thank you Maritou. Somehow, I know that you will make a difference. Say, can you spare a few moments to talk about some personal matters."

"Sure! And I'll bring you up to date on the situation with Rayloh and Naomi."

A few moments later, they were alone, conversing over the unfathomable distance of one hundred and fifty light years but, in a way, face to face.

"You know, it's ironic," Gar began. "You and Rayloh were together for a while—you know, with him being my clone, and I've been with my Maritou, your double, for these three hundred years."

"Yes, those things cross my thoughts quite often," she confessed.

"Now that Rena has been found, Maritou is worried that she might lose me. I've tried to reassure her that I am totally committed to her. Because you understand the way she thinks and feels, maybe you can offer some advice."

"Gar? She has the memories of the time that you met Rena and me. Although I never had you, she experienced the grief I felt over the fact that my love for you would go unsatisfied, forever. Those thoughts and feelings must be strongly triggered by the present circumstances, and it is only natural for her to be scared. Right now, she has her hands full and has pushed this threat to the back of her mind. But once she has triumphed over the situation on the Armada, those feelings will come flooding back. You will need to be understanding."

"That makes sense."

"Before we sign off," Venahus said, "there have been some surprising developments. Rayloh and Naomi elected to receive your and Rena's memories and they are adjusting very quickly. Rayloh insists on going on the raid to free Rena."

"And you have agreed to let him go? He must be adapting very quickly. But he has no combat experience and, if Sten goes too, that leaves only one spot for you or le Noir."

'It's going to be cramped, but we have managed to have one of the crates modified to carry both Sten and le Noir. So, the four of us will go. And you are right, Rayloh is adjusting very quickly. Having the combined knowledge of Rayloh and the learning that you possessed fifteen hundred years ago, his overall functions have improved. He is still adapting to differences in values and emotional bonds but, other than that, he's 100%."

"How is Naomi doing?"

"She is also doing fairly well. The Rena part is on-board with the fact that Rena will be reunited with the part of Rayloh that is you, basically. However, the Naomi part is having some mixed feelings."

"I'm just wondering why Naomi is not joining the mission instead of Rayloh? Gar wondered. "Her being equipped with Rena's combat experience would give the rescue team a better advantage."

"It's that Naomi is not ready for combat. She's having a value struggle. The Naomi part is strongly opposed to the use of violence."

"I see."

"I have to go, now, Gar. I will get back to you after I analyze the data on W-292."

"Thanks, Maritou."

Chapter 24

MC3

Maritou called Cole to her office. She and Lore Li had been studying the radar flight reports and camera footage from the Indersol Group.

"What have you learned?" Cole asked.

"Look at this, Chief," Lore Li directed as she brought up images of the Indersol 'Tube'. "You're looking at The Tube, a corridor that services the entire array. It was designed for efficiency and connects all three asteroids of the group. This means that the array can share a common shuttle port and allows lively interaction between the various businesses that are located there. It's good for commerce."

After a few moments, the corridor images went fuzzy.

"This static lasts long enough for someone to come out of the shuttle port and disappear into any one of the facilities within the array," Lore Li continued. "We tracked Vin's assassins here to Indersol. The interruption in the surveillance cameras occurred shortly after their arrival. When the images cleared up, there was no sign of them."

"What about the maintenance vehicle they used?" Cole asked.

"It's still there in the hangar."

"We believe that they made this stop to trick us into focusing on Indersol," Maritou declared. "They were just there to change their disguises and leave a cold trail. But they weren't counting on Lore Li. Even though they each took indirect routes from there, she managed to track them all the way to MC3."

"Maybe it's time we raid MC3," Cole declared. "Are your strike forces ready, Maritou?"

"We could use another day or two of planning and training. I've added a squad of bot handlers, led by Lieutenant du Mantahn. And I've just returned from a meeting with my demolition team. They are exploring ways to break open the air lock."

She walked to the lead board and pointed to a photo of the MerCon array which showed all three asteroids of the group: MC1, MC2, and MC3.

"MC3 has only one port and it is here," she indicated, "on the far edge of the asteroid. The main assault group will be focused there and, as they force the air lock, two two-man teams will attempt to enter through the emergency hatches which are located here—and here, on the sides of MC3."

"But you would be going in with such a small contingent," Cole warned.

"That's all that will fit in the air lock and the emergency hatch extracting units. The demolition crew is training to open the air lock hatch without destroying it. That way, a second wave can gain access once the air lock is cleared. But this will take precious time. That's why I hope to surprise them by also coming through the emergency hatches."

"We could just cut off their supplies and wait them out," Cole suggested. He was having second thoughts.

"We could do that, but imagine the risks," Maritou argued. "The Mission's critical supplies of plasma engines and incubators are in there. If those were to be sabotaged, it could mean the end of the entire Mission."

"I see," Cole conceded.

"We can aim for readiness in two days," Maritou proposed. "Let's confer with Arohn. He could lead a surprise raid on the Dulamar facilities at the same time, while your team is making arrests of suspected conspirators.

Cole looked at his watch. "You should leave, soon, Maritou. Mihn is expecting you."

"Ok, please set up a meeting with Gar. Maybe he can see us early in the morning, before he meets with the Council."

Chapter 25

The Letter

Maritou arrived at Mihn's apartment in time to set the table before Mihn came home. She brought Kornunah Bread and a hearty soup.

Mihn came in and sniffed the spicy fragrance. "What a delightful aroma."

"Sit down and have some, before it gets cold."

"This soup is fabulous," Mihn exclaimed.

"You'll have to give Dar Enock the credit for the soup," Maritou confessed. "It's made mostly from her herb and vegetable creations."

"I haven't seen Dar for centuries," Mihn reflected. "She was one of my strongest supporters when I started, and the very first grower to use the Rovabots.

"When I ordered the soup," Maritou apologized, "I had hoped to stay here longer. But things have changed, and I must get back early, tonight. That's why I broke my promise and didn't bring any Vernah Berries. But I will, one day soon."

"I see that you have brought something for me," Mihn said, indicating the case that Maritou had placed by the desk.

"Yes, I'll explain that after you finish your soup. I've also brought you a surprise."

"Can't wait!" Mihn beamed.

After dinner, Maritou explained the attack on Vin and showed Mihn the sample of attack bots she had taken from du Ouht.

"Your worst fears were well founded," Maritou revealed. She passed the swarming container to Mihn. "There are so many unknowns when it comes to these bots, I'm wondering if you would take them and find out what you can."

"You need not even ask."

"What we need to know, most urgently, is how effective your Rovabots are at killing these attack bots, and how much protection we can expect. We can fight more effectively if we Gentar don't have to wear protective suits that cover our wings. And, as of yet, we don't have a way to protect them without a full body suit. We need to fly."

How many are in this swarming container? Mihn asked.

"Five. And here is a dead one with the helmet still attached. Will that help?"

"Yes! From the dead one, maybe I can isolate the type of venom used. If there is an antivenom available, you could carry a syringe with you in case of a successful attack."

"That would be most helpful," Maritou told her. "I expect we will see some action, day after tomorrow. Thanks to your help, we have a much better chance of success."

"I will also test the effectiveness of the Rovabots by having them attack this sample," said Mihn. "To do this, I need to estimate the size of the swarm used to kill Vin."

Picking up the swarming vessel, Mihn asked, "Is this the same size of swarming vessel the assassins used?"

"Yes."

"Okay, I can estimate the size of the swarm and use these five for a test. I may only get one shot at it because they may all be killed in the test. I think I can have results for you by tomorrow, along with a formula for an effective antivenom. I'll go back to my lab, after you leave, so I can work undisturbed."

"Good! Now, I promised you a surprise, remember?"

"Oh, yes!"

Maritou handed Mihn a letter from Cole. It carried his initials on the seal.

"I think you have been waiting for this for a long time," Maritou beamed mischievously.

Mihn took the letter and held it to her breast. "Yes, I have!"

Chapter 26

Moshadan Rule

Director Ashura BoKeed stood and addressed the full Council.

"A matter has come to light that requires our immediate consideration. Two days ago, after lengthy discussions regarding the selection of new worlds for habitation, we voted almost unanimously to commit the Mission to W-292. We made this decision based upon years of scientific study which points to W-292 as an ideal candidate. Information is now surfacing that questions the very validity of the evidence we've relied upon. "

The gasps that broke out in the Chamber quickly turned into an outcry. Several councilpersons rose in protest.

"What is the meaning of this outrage?" Mi Dulamar roared.

A loud commotion broke out throughout the chamber.

"Order!" BoKeed demanded.

His direction was ignored. Several members were huddled around Dulamar, and the pandemonium continued until Dulamar raised his hands. He was clearly in-charge at the moment.

"I move to ratify our original vote on this matter without further discussion," he pressed.

Senior Councilwoman, Uma de Corsa, stood and quickly protested.

"Just a moment!" She demanded. "Let's be clear that there is no need to reverse our decision without a discussion. I have looked at the evidence and we just need a little time to understand its significance. It may not be advisable to announce our decision, today. We should delay the announcement and the ratification until we know more."

"We don't have time to delay," Dulamar insisted. "We have only this small window of opportunity and the crew cannot be kept in the dark."

"There's a chance we might reverse our decision. How would that go over if we announce prematurely?" Uma challenged. "I am invoking the Moshadan Rule."

Most of the Councilmembers had no idea what the Moshadan Rule meant. It had never come into play during their terms of office. The rule required the Council to move into closed session testimony and discussion before any votes could be taken.

But Dulamar knew the rule.

"That rule is antiquated," He protested. "It requires the existence of a serious security threat, and there is none."

"Here, here!" The Speaker broke in. "There may very well be such a threat. And the rule, when invoked, is automatic. We must now move to closed session until the matter is addressed. Only then are we allowed to entertain any motions from the floor. At this time, I ask that any non-council members clear this chamber. And the press is ordered to delay any publication of these proceedings."

There continued to be much grumbling as the Chamber was cleared, but the puzzlement over the Moshadan Rule had quieted the heated protests. Nobody wanted to appear ignorant of the rules.

"I hereby call to order this closed session of Council," BoKeed announced. "Councilwoman de Corsa, please call your witnesses."

"I call the Chairman of the Intelligence Committee, Akai Halron."

Halron came forward and was seated in the witness box.

"Chairman Halron," Uma began, "have you been briefed regarding the arrest of Colonel Ben Ru?"

A wave of astonishment swept the chamber. News of Ben Ru's arrest had not been released.

"Order!" BoKeed demanded and, this time, he was obeyed. "I ask that you all remain quiet throughout this session and listen to the testimony. Madam de Corsa, you may proceed."

"I'll repeat the question. Have you been briefed by Mission Security regarding the arrest of Ben Ru?"

"Yes, I have," he answered.

"Please tell us what you have learned."

"He is accused of assaulting Co-Commander Gar Lahn and attempting to murder Maritou le Rohn. He had an accomplice, Sauhn Lin who has confessed."

"Is that all?" Uma probed, doubtfully.

"Well, no. Sauhn Lin contends that Ben Ru is involved with several others in a conspiracy to take over the Mission. He has named other conspirators whose identities have yet to be divulged to the Committee."

Despite BoKeed's warning, an outbreak of disbelieving cries swept the chamber.

BoKeed allowed this and waited until it subsided somewhat before he intervened. "Order! Councilwoman de Corsa, please continue."

"Has the Committee been informed of any matters concerning evidence of tampering regarding the W-292 data?" Uma asked.

"No."

"That is all I have for this witness," she said.

"The floor is open for members to cross-examine Chairman Halron," BoKeed offered.

He waited a few moments but there were no takers.

"Chairman Halron, you are excused. Madam de Corsa, do you have any further witnesses?"

"I call Co-Commander de Vul."

An aide left the chamber momentarily, and returned with Arohn, who had not appeared earlier in the day. Arohn crossed the chamber and took his seat in the witness chair.

"Commander de Vul, please tell us what you know in relation to possible tampering of scientific data regarding solar system W-292 and its planets."

"Yes. After the arrest of Ben Ru, our security forces performed a thorough search of his facilities in the Centex Group. They found nothing at first, until a hidden office was discovered where they found photographs and infrared images of the W-292 planets that appear remarkably different from the set that the Council has been given."

"And how are they different?"

Arohn pulled a memory pearl from his pocket. "This contains images of the two data sets. If they can be displayed, I'll show you."

He handed her the pearl.

"I think we can do that."

She called for an aide and gave him instructions. He went to the media room to load the pearl and momentarily returned with a remote which he handed to Arohn.

A large screen came down from the ceiling. Arohn flipped through the photos, stopping on side-by-side photographs of a planet.

These are images of W292b, the second planet from W-292's star," he explained. "The images are identical in many respects except the one on the right, which was found in the secret office, has features that are clearly different from the one on the left."

"What does that prove?" Dulamar shouted. "Maybe the planet has rotated and we are looking at two different sides."

"Keep your questions for cross examination," BoKeed warned.

"No, I think he is making a good point," Uma put forth. "Commander, please explain."

"Well, let's look a little closer," Arohn said, and he zoomed in on the upper margins of the photos. "Look at the image identifiers here at the top. They are the same. These images are different versions of the same photo."

Arohn paused to let the clamor subside. This time, BoKeed let the commotion die down, allowing the implications to take root.

Uma, anticipating the next challenge from Dulamar, stole his thunder.

"And, so what does this tell us, Commander? What does it prove?"

"I've looked at all of the photos and infrared images, as have others. But none of us are planetary astronomers, and we cannot rely on the Centex team at the moment, because any one of them could be involved in the deception. We just don't know yet."

Dulamar piped in again. One side of his upper lip pulled up in a snarl.

"With all respect, Commander, that doesn't help. We are committed to W-292 colonization, and we need to alter our course right now! I move that we put a stop to this nonsense. And if you are going to stand in the way—let me remind you—we, the Council call the shots, not you. And you can be replaced at any time."

"I must object to that," Uma charged forth calmly. "We'll get to a discussion in due time. Right now, I don't believe that Commander de Vul is finished. So, Commander, since you are not qualified to analyze this data, what do you propose?"

"Co-Commander Gar Lahn has enlisted help from Maritou Venahus who is presently on Hogar. She is a leading authority on planetary science, and he has sent her the data. She is expected to have some answers by tomorrow."

One of the Vulan councilwomen stood and addressed the assembly. "May I ask a question, Speaker BoKeed?"

BoKeed looked to Uma for objections.

"Go right ahead, I think I am about finished," Uma stated.

"Commander? We have always trusted you as our chief navigator. Do you agree that, if we don't start the deceleration sequence right away, we will lose our opportunity to achieve an ideal orbiting position close to the target planets of W-292?"

"Years ago, when the mission became interested in W-292," Arohn explained, "we calculated a range of alternative trajectories looking for an optimal balance of safety, resource economy, timing, and the desired orbit. The currently proposed trajectory seems to be focused mainly on getting the Armada into orbital position in the least amount of time. It calls for a direct approach to the solar system, rather than a spiraling entry that would take more time but would take advantage of gravity assist deceleration and be 78 percent more fuel efficient. The direct entry would entail a lot more risk to safety and a massive depletion of resources—especially our reserves of helium fuel. The proposed plan calls for a maximum rate of deceleration which will basically drain that resource."

"Would you say more about your safety concerns, Commander," the councilwoman asked.

"We have over 50 arrays and single asteroids in the Armada. Each one requires its own set of helium engines, and positioning everything into orbit will require a delicate ballet of synchronicity. If there is even one system failure, anything could happen. Moreover, we don't really know what lies in our path. We are still so far away from W-292, we won't be able to spot small asteroids that may be in our way until it is too late."

The councilwoman turned and addressed her constituents. "Why have we gotten into such a damn hurry? And why were our commanders left out on this critical decision?"

The chamber went silent and motionless for a long moment.

"I move that—" the councilwoman began, but was cut off by BoKeed.

"We will hold our motions until the testimony is over and have adequately discussed the issues. Procedure will be followed."

The councilwoman took her seat and BoKeed told Uma that she could continue.

"I have no more questions, and Commander de Vul is my final witness."

"The floor is open for cross examination," BoKeed announced.

Dulamar inhaled and his mouth opened for a heated reprisal. But something he suddenly felt inside, stopped him. It was the memory of the humiliation he'd suffered the last time he challenged de Vul and lost. Remembering how, when attempting to denounce Mihn Rova, de Vul had outmaneuvered him. He wisely remained silent and took his chair.

"Thank you, Commander," BoKeed said. "Keep us apprised of any news from Maritou Venahus and stand by for our decision."

"I will." Arohn nodded and walked out of the chamber.

Gar, summoned to the radio, spoke with Venahus. "You have answers for us already?"

"I decided to change my approach," she told him. "My first instinct was to just assume that the official photos had been manipulated and to focus on the differences. But, as soon as I started looking at them, it became clear what the deception was all about. So I decided to find evidence of deliberate doctoring. And even though these are very professional fakes, the differences are so extreme that even the best forger would leave telltale signs. There are several subtle features that point to this, but the most distinctive are the dark side edges of the planets. When they removed the lights from the outside curvatures, they had to fashion artificial edges which are almost impossible to create convincingly. When I zoomed in, the deception was easy to spot. I'm sending you a report you can take to the Council."

"That will help immensely. From what Arohn tells me, the Council is very skeptical and feeling pressured. But tell me—what do the real images reveal—the lights?"

"Civilization!"

"That was our concern. What is it about the images that points to civilization?"

"The lights are concentrated along coastlines and there appear to be many rivers that are outlined with a sprinkling of lights. And the infrared evidence gives us a clue as to why radio wave activity has not been detected."

"Yes?"

"They simply don't have the technology, yet. The lights on the larger planet, in particular, must be fueled by some type of gas because they burn at a different temperature than electric lights. And only the largest cities of the smaller planet have some electric lights which indicates that they are, just now, entering an age of scientific advancement. But the inhabitants of both worlds appear to be thriving."

"And an invasion from us could take that all away from them. And they won't even know we've arrived. They might have telescopes but, if someone spots us, to them we will just be a newly discovered assortment of asteroids. I'll take this to the Council when they convene in the morning. De Vul will be too busy to go. Thank you, Maritou!"

Chapter 27

Supernova

With Maritou at the controls and Lieutenant Mantahn strapped in behind her in the emergency hatch extracting unit, they spotted the MerCon asteroids. Ahead of them, leading the assault, was the initial strike team that would enter through the main airlock of MC3.

Arohn and his forces were carrying out a simultaneous raid on the Dulamar facilities at Solay Mahn. So Maritou's team would not have backup for some time.

Without warning, there was a massive explosion of light!

"What was that?" Mantahn cried.

As their eyes adjusted to the increasing intensity, they spotted the source. A large ball of light floated just off the starboard side of MC3.

"A supernova!" Maritou exclaimed. "I've seen a few of them, but never at the moment of explosion."

Maritou called her strike team leader. "In case you don't realize what just happened, Captain Bakari, that explosion did not come from MC3. It was a supernova. As you make your approach, position your ship in the shadow of the astcroid."

"Yes ma'am! Making course correction, now. The team is ready."

Captain Ambar Bakari was an Abaru. As a reserve officer, she had trained with Maritou whenever her unit was called up. Her combat skills approached the level of Maritou's and she was a quick thinking and effective leader.

"It seems so strange—you know, the supernova," she exclaimed to Maritou. "Do you think it's an omen?"

"I'm not a believer in omens, Ambar, but who really knows? Let's just call it a good sign."

Maritou moved into position above one of the emergency hatches and ordered Lieutenant Simi, the other extraction unit officer, to wait outside the other emergency hatch. They would wait until the main assault unit was inside the air lock and drawing the defenses of the enemy before they began their docking maneuvers.

Finally, the agreed upon time had elapsed and it was time for Maritou and Simi to make their move. Spinning in lock step with the asteroid, the crews of the emergency extraction units were now experiencing gravity once again as they carried out their docking procedures. Maritou opened the pressure valve on the hatch to equalize the pressure inside the rescue unit with that of the warehouse inside. "Now, let's see what is waiting for us in there."

She opened the inspection tube and pushed a camera probe through the hatch. The exit platform on the inside was empty. But the platform was at the end of a short hallway which turned to the left and the probe would not extend far enough to see around the bend. The probe's microphone was only picking up the sound of its own cable sliding through the inspection tube.

"It looks clear," she told Mantahn as she extracted the cable. "Ready?"

"Ready!"

She radioed the other extraction unit team who were also ready to venture inside. Then she released the hatch. The hinges squealed as it swung open. Mantahn released a swarm to protect their vulnerable wings and they crawled out onto the platform, weapons at the ready.

Maritou peered around the corner. Finding the hallway empty, she rushed to the far end. Just before she reached it, the sound of the battle, below, began echoing through the upper levels.

That's odd. It shouldn't have taken that long for them to engage.

When Captain Bakari and her assault team entered the air lock, they were surprised to find the inner hatch open and no sign of resistance beyond. She could see the service elevator straight ahead. Giant plasma engines were lined up to the sides and behind the elevator shaft. The warehouse was totally silent.

"They're waiting to ambush us," she told her lieutenants. "Position the shields and have the swarm handlers stand by. Don't deploy the heavy machine guns, for the moment. They would surely damage the plasma engines, which the enemy has placed there as a shield. Anti-personnel armor piercing rounds will have to do."

She ordered a small group of Vulan troops to advance behind a shield. They inched ahead slowly beyond the inner hatch and into a large open area. The space was open to the level above, which had two large open galleries connected by catwalks.

We're dead meat out there! She grated silently.

She pulled back her scouts.

"We can't tiptoe out there," she told her officers. "Our heavy shields are useless the way they are, because they don't protect us from fire coming from overhead. But I have a plan. Bring up the machine guns. And see if there are any mechanics among us."

The two machine guns were quickly wheeled out. She had them removed from their carriages in order to mount the shields for protection from an overhead assault. The demolition team had everything needed to make the conversion. The machine guns were then remounted vertically through holes burned through the centers of the shields. The shields were wide enough to accommodate an additional hole on each end to mount light machine guns. Vulan gunners were chosen because their modified body armor provided full protection from the swarms that would surely be deployed.

"The machine gun modifications will give us a slim element of surprise, so we must act quickly. The machine guns will draw immediate fire, and the Gentars will take wing at the sound of the first shot. Handlers, release your swarms! Gunners, move!"

The brief moment of surprise delayed the counter attack long enough to allow the gunners to reach a favorable position where they drew the enemy fire for a few moments while the Gentars flew above the catwalks. It looked like the tide was definitely turning in favor of Ambar and her unit. Then came the swarms of flying killers. But Mihn's Rovabots were proving to be effective, and the Gentars were suffering only a limited number of stings, lessening the effect of the venom.

But the Gentars were being picked off by gunfire, one by one. Captain Bakari, flying above a cat walk, spotted places in the galleries to gain cover. Her high frequency whistle signaled her troops to follow suit as she flew into a gallery.

From her sheltered position she noticed strange things about the enemy soldiers. Their faces were monstrous and they all looked the same—like giant attack bots. Then, when she focused on their fallen comrades, she could see that they were all Vulans. Some of their hoods had fallen off as they fell. It was the hoods that had given them a grotesque look.

The firing stopped and she heard her gunners celebrating the victory. The shields had worked. There were no more living enemy soldiers in the galleries and on the catwalks.

Her swarm of Defenderbots had dwindled noticeably. And for the moment, the survivors were being picked off.

Ambar began to feel drowsy from the few bites she had received. There were three syringes of antivenom in her vest and she gave herself an injection. Then, she came out of her defensive position and walked to the nearest catwalk to assess the casualties to her troops. The battle had been costly. She counted seven down—six Gentar and one gunner. Four were being treated by the Vulan medics. She called down to the lead medic.

"Sergeant, what's the status?"

"Three dead, Captain, and we are treating one gunner with a ricochet wound, one Gentar with a shattered wing and a concussion, and two being treated with antivenom. Looks like they will pull through."

She addressed the gunners. "Gunners, secure the lower level and meet me here at Level Two. There is a stairwell behind the plasma engines."

She had four winged warriors left, and they joined her on the catwalk. All four had given themselves injections and three were fit enough for the next task of securing the upper levels. The fourth had a minor bullet wound to his shooting arm, and she sent him below, to the medics.

"Now we move up, one level at a time," she ordered. "Follow me."

They walked to the back gallery and prepared to enter the main staircase. From the opposite gallery, they heard the bang of a door flying open as two Vulan monsters positioned their machine gun in the doorway. Then, came the insidious buzzing of a fresh wave of attack bots.

There was no time to call for more Defenderbots. They would never reach them in time.

"Hit the floor!" she ordered.

They all carried nets to put over their vulnerable wings when the Defenderbots failed. She grabbed her own and, before she turned to face a hail of bullets, she had it draped over her comrades.

Then, the rattle of the machine gun and her world went dark.

Maritou carried a machine pistol but, for the moment, she had to move with stealth and would rely on her bow.

The emergency hatches opened out into the middle of the asteroid which meant she was standing in the largest section of the warehouse. The level was filled with used mining equipment, and her view of Lieutenant Simi, on the other side, was blocked. He had orders to remain hidden and protect Maritou from the rear as she made her way down to surprise the enemy from behind.

Maritou took wing and began her controlled decent toward the battle that raged below. For Gentars, flying at low velocity more or less straight down, is more like parachuting. She went feet first, floating down the stairwell.

When she was half-way down, the gunfire below faded and then stopped. She paused on Level Four to listen and advanced with more caution. From the stairwell landing, just above Level Three, Mantahn caught up with her and they heard voices but could not discern whether it was the enemy or their own troops.

Then, someone was moving on Level Three. They watched as an enemy swarm handler stepped into view in the stairwell. He toted a very large swarming vessel and released its deadly contents before Maritou's arrow penetrated the gap between his body armor and his helmet. A cloud of attack bots was descending on Bakari's unit!

"Release all the Defenderbots!" Maritou ordered Mantahn, and she took wing in a head-down dive through the stairwell. She would catch up with the deadly cloud of attack bots, if she could. Her defenders, attracted to her wristband might have a chance to wipe it out.

Reaching Level Two, she came face to face with an odd-looking pair that had their machine gun trained on something Maritou could not see on the other side of the wall. She took them both out with her machine pistol, but not before their weapon erupted in a rapid-fire barrage.

When she made it to the doorway, she saw Amber reeling from the attack and falling. She had been shot and an angry cloud was raining down its deadly pellets upon her. Maritou's protectors had caught up with her, and she flew to Amber and covered her with her own body and outstretched wings. Amber was unconscious but still alive.

Mantahn arrived and covered them with a net. The other Gentars had signaled for more defenders which arrived. Slowly, the number of attackers dwindled and the death-dealing cloud evaporated.

The medics arrived and tended to Amber who had been grazed in the head. She was given more antivenom.

Maritou had surprisingly few bites and didn't need anything. Before she left for the raid, Gar insisted that she rub on some concoction he had developed back when he and O'Ruhn lived in huts on Hogar.

"It kept most of the flies off when we were out hunting," He contended. "It stinks like crap, though."

"So, this just your way of telling Mantahn to keep his hands to himself?" she'd retorted.

"I don't want anything biting my woman."

Maritou walked over to the two dead machine gunners. Puzzled, she inspected one of the helmets that had fallen off when she shot them.

"It's a circuit board that's been folded into a helmet," she said out loud.

It was still attached by wires coming through the scull.

"These two look like twins," she said, surprised.

"They look just like the others that we killed," one of Amber's winged soldiers informed her.

Maritou gathered the warriors and briefed them on the next phase of their operation. She picked out three of the Gentars and half of the Vulans to come with her to secure the upper levels of the asteroid.

"The rest of you stay here to guard the wounded and clean things up. Any questions? Okay, let's move!"

Chapter 28

The Labyrinth of King Minos

One hundred and fifty light-years away, it was time to get into the crates.

Sten said goodbye to Deek, his friend that was risking everything to help. Deek worked for the supply house that procured provisions for O'Ruhn's vessel.

If the mission failed, the rescue team would probably all die quickly in a fight to take over the ship. But Deek would surely meet an unspeakable end.

"These crates are amazing," Deek observed. He hadn't been informed of the exact plans. All he knew was to meet them at the loading dock in the middle of the night.

In the early hours of the morning, a light cargo pulled up to the dock. It was disguised as a sanitation vessel. The crates were inside. A team of Arohn's men swapped crates of supplies with identical looking ones and transferred as many of the supplies as would fit into the crates where the invaders would be concealed. Each of the replacement crates had a false bottom and sliding panels providing access to hidden compartments.

"The crates were Sten's idea," Rayloh told Deek, and turned to Sten giving him a playful jab. "It's time to climb into our nests. Thank you,

Deek. And be careful. If all goes well, we'll see you soon."

They opened their compartments and slid inside feet first. Deek handed them each their weapons and equipment and closed the panels. Soon, they heard the voices of the dock workers arriving and then the drone of the supply ship pulling into position.

Rayloh's crate jerked sharply as it was hoisted by the loader, causing him to fart loudly.

"Was that you?" one of the workers asked his companion.

"No, it was probably something shifting in the load."

He yelled at the loader operator. "Hey! Be careful!"

As the crate was jockeyed into position, the odor escaped.

"Oh! A container has broken open. What do they eat down there on the ship?"

"Yah! Blame it on the cargo. What did you eat last night?"

The other laughed. "Question is, what did you eat?"

The rest of the cargo was loaded and, a short time later, the supply ship descended into the murky depths. Next stop, the floating fortress and the battle to come.

Once they reached the flagship, the process was slow. The first thing Rayloh noticed was that the air was stale. The receiving crew were bickering and not making much progress. Rayloh strained to hold in the gas that was building in his gut.

One of the workers was complaining about their working conditions. "Every time he gets into one of his states, someone gets killed."

His coworker held up a hand of caution, stepping momentarily into the corridor, checking for passers-by. "Quiet, or you'll get both of us skewered."

"Rumor has it that, this time, it's because of something his son has done."

"Silence!" the other warned. "Say no more to me. I want to keep my manhood. Now finish up here, and I'll go submit the shipping documents."

The remaining worker continued to unload the cargo, muttering to himself.

Rayloh lost his battle with the increasing gas pressure. A large amount escaped with an almost silent "PHOO." Silent, yes. Odorless, no.

"My brother's wife and stepchildren!" the worker swore angrily. "What the—"

Knowing they had been discovered, Rayloh crawled out of his crate.

"What have we here? Is this some kind of trick?" exclaimed the worker. He turned quickly to fetch help, but came face to face with Sten.

"Where are you going in such a hurry?"

Startled, the man's jaw opened as if to scream. Sten grabbed him, cupping his hand over the mouth, but his voice was calm and reassuring. "Don't scream. We won't hurt you. Okay?" Sten nodded. "Okay?"

The man oriented himself to the situation and started nodding back. Sten maintained his grip but removed his hand.

"Okay now? You're not going to scream?"

"Okay!"

"I heard you talking to your coworker. It sounds like you live in fear here, don't you? We are here to help."

"We?"

"Yes. There are four of us. Come on out, everyone."

The worker apparently didn't recognize Sten.

Maritou's hand appeared from the bottom of her crate, stacking her weapons to one side. When Arohn appeared, the worker was not alarmed. He was quite familiar with Vulans, who made up a large percentage of the ship's crew.

The worker reached out suddenly, for a button on the wall and Maritou grabbed him before he could reach it.

"It's just an exhaust fan," he cried. "I thought you were going to trust me?" he said, somewhat offended.

Rayloh's odor was starting to reach Sten. "Does that fan have a high speed?" he chuckled.

"I've seen you a few times in the dining room," Sten told the worker. "What is your name?"

"JoDan. I am JoDan," he said with some new found pride. He was not used to being talked to as if he was somehow not just a lowly servant.

"I'm Sten. This is Maritou, Arohn and Rayloh."

Arohn stepped forward. "Right now, we could use your help, JoDan."

"Sure! What do I need to do?"

"We need to make our way to the main disposal facility. There are plenty of places to conceal ourselves, there, and we will have access to anywhere on the vessel."

Arohn continued giving instructions to JoDan while the others inventoried the supplies and weapons and stowed them in packs.

"Ready?" Arohn prompted. Let's go."

JoDan went ahead, pointing out places where the invaders could conceal themselves as he made his way down a corridor. As he reached key locations, he gave the come ahead signal. Soon, they were safely inside the disposal facility.

"That was the easy part." Arohn said. "Security will be tight wherever we go from here."

"Well done, JoDan," Sten praised. "Now, please go back and find Jamah and send him here. He is an old friend of mine and can be trusted. Do you know him?"

"Yes, he's the head butler. I'll need to check in at the supply office, first, or they will send someone to find me. Then, I'll go find Jamah.

"Okay, just don't take any chances," said Arohn. "After you find Jamah, how will we contact you if we need something?"

"I'll go back to my quarters. Use any wall phone and just enter J-O-D-A-N."

JoDan hesitated. He wanted to ask his new friends something, but decided it could wait. He had only been to the bubble islands once, training in the operation and maintenance of new cargo lifts. The feel of the sun and the fresh air in his lungs was forever after etched vividly in his memories. For the first and only time, he was able to fly free, soaring over the strange and wonderful world of his ancestors.

He wanted his new friends to take him back. "I'll do anything I can to help you out."

"In that case," said Arohn, "don't go back to your quarters. After you find Jamah, come back here and bring yourself a sanitation workers uniform. I have a plan."

After JoDan left, there was little to do but wait and rest.

"Okay, we are on track," Arohn said, reviewing their objectives. "The first thing we'll do is neutralize the security office and the surveillance cameras. That will be my job. JoDan will get me there, hidden inside a sanitation cart. Then, when Jamah arrives here, we'll find out where O'Ruhn is, and work out a plan for our attack. Any questions, so far?"

"Rena," Rayloh exclaimed. "We must keep her safe."

"She has pretty much the run of the ship," Sten informed them. "If we get word to her, she could find a good hiding spot for herself."

"Why don't we just call her?" Arohn suggested, looking at Rayloh with fond mischief.

Rayloh could only nod agreement, his identity as Gar struggling to reconcile his feelings between the original Rena and the newly awakened Rena inside Naomi. And for Gar, whose memories ended even before Rena was kidnapped, no time at all had passed since he and Rena were together.

But Rena has endured fifteen hundred years of captivity. How has she changed?

Rayloh thought, too, about the Gar on the Armada who had also experienced all those centuries separated from the one he loved.

Who belongs to who? And how does one relate to their loved one that has endured so much, while they themselves have not?

Across the room, the phone rang, shocking Rayloh back to the moment at hand. Two rings and then silence, the signal to pick up when the phone sounded again.

Arohn answered when it did. "Yes? . . . Okay, see you then."

Arohn shared the news with the others. "He's found Jamah, who will be here, shortly. JoDan is coming separately."

"Let's call Rena, now. Sten," Maritou said. "Would you do that? Let her know you have come back with help and then I'll talk with her."

The four of them huddled around the phone as Sten entered the number.

"Lady Rena's chamber," answered Henovar, Rena's companion.

"Hi! This is Sten. Please ask Rena to come to the phone."

"Sorry, Sten, Lady Rena is resting and cannot be disturbed."

"This is urgent!"

"Maybe if you call back tomorrow—"

Arohn took the phone and his Vulan voice boomed. "This is BarOak!" he lied. "Put Rena on the phone or I'll come up there myself and devour you!"

After a silent pause, "This is Rena. Sten, is that you?"

Arohn gave the receiver back to Sten.

"Rena, this is Sten."

"Sten! Are you back? How—"

"Yes! I've come back with help to free you."

"Are you sure? You must be careful!"

"Yes, but we are prepared. Everything is in motion but you may come into danger once our presence is revealed. You must get yourself to a safe hiding place. The security cameras will be disabled, soon. We'll give you another call to let you know when."

"Sten? You will not be able to take your father alive. Are you ready for that?"

"I only know that he must be stopped. I'll deal with my feelings, later. Rena, there is someone with me that wants to talk to you. Here she is."

"Maritou, that must be you!" she guessed.

"Rena!"

"I knew you would come for me one day, Maritou. I have never eliminated that thought. I have just suppressed it with my meditations. I couldn't allow anything to obsess me or I would have lost my mind."

"Until a few weeks ago, we didn't know where you were or that you were alive."

"I knew it would take time. But you are here. Somehow, I think that things cannot move into place until the time is right." Rena hesitated. "And what of Gar?" she managed cautiously.

"Your Gar is still on the Armada, searching for a new home."

"I knew he still lived! Rena exclaimed. "I can feel it."

"He knows we are here to rescue you. He's waiting to hear word of your escape."

"How can that be? They must be light years away."

Maritou explained the Quantum Two-Way to Rena. "You see, space does not exist between the intertwined particles produced at each end, and the communication is instantaneous. My Copy and Arohn de Vul developed it."

"Well, what took them so long?" Rena chuckled.

"It's good to hear my dear friend laughing."

Maritou turned serious. "Rena?" She knew that the next words she spoke would stir Rena's heart. But she must be prepared. "I have someone else with me. Your Gar is far away—"

"But you have his replica with you!"

"Yes!"

Maritou waited through a very long pause and could hear Rena crying quietly. "Maritou, tell him I'm not ready to speak with him right now. We will have much to share when this is over, and I need a little time to prepare myself."

"He will understand. I will call you when the cameras are disabled. Then, go to a safe place and we will find you when the excitement is over."

"Maritou!" Rena's voice was urgent. "You must hurry! I didn't tell Sten, but his fiancée Anya was arrested. I fear that O'Ruhn has wicked plans for her. He keeps saying that he is going to teach Sten a lesson."

Maritou glanced at her timepiece. "Do you know where O'Ruhn will be when the sun is in the seventh arc? That is our earliest estimate of when we will strike. We are waiting for Jamah and JoDan to arrive.

"He's generally in the salon at that time, preparing himself for the evening orgies. So, you may be in time to save Anya. I'll ready myself and wait to hear from you."

After the call, Rena noticed her feelings were reawakening, after centuries of self-regulation. Fear was beginning to pass through her in waves. Today would mark either her freedom, or most likely, the end of her existence.

Rayloh gave Maritou a questioning look.

"The two of you will talk when this is over," Maritou said. "She needs a little time to adjust to the idea that her Gar is out of reach and that you are here."

"I feel confused myself. It is hard to explain, but—"

"Don't even try, my friend," interjected Arohn. "Things may come into focus for you when our task here is finished."

They settled in for some rest and nourishment, awaiting the arrivals of Jamah and JoDan.

JoDan arrived first and Arohn set about briefing him on their operation.

"We now have information to believe that O'Ruhn will be in his chambers, so I have decided not to return here, and we will meet the others in the Abaru baths. We can get access to O'Ruhn's private corridor through the supply closet. That's where your task will end."

Arohn checked the time. "Six and a half arcs."

Jamah had still not arrived.

"We may have to go for it without Jamah," Arohn said as he concealed himself and his weapons inside the cleaning cart.

Meanwhile, JoDan drew a map showing an alternate route in case the baths proved to be a problem.

"This way may take a little longer, but usually, there are no guards down below through the service corridor. These stairs here empty out in the hallway leading to the Ceremonial Chamber, which will be on the right. There are always guards in the hallway."

"Check your timepieces," Arohn told everyone." I now have six arcs, thirty-three and twenty. We want the element of surprise. Wait until I call you and make your way quickly. If I haven't called by six seventy, leave here and go by the alternate route. If there is no resistance, enter the hallway at exactly six eighty-five and maybe we can catch the guards in our crossfire. Otherwise, we'll meet you in the baths and go in, together. JoDan, let's go."

Arohn closed the curtain on the maintenance cart and JoDan

wasted no time getting them to the security center. He positioned the cart where it partially blocked the door and rang the bell. The guard that came to the door looked contemptuously at JoDan.

"What are you doing here? We won't need anything until the next shift," he said and tried to slam the door.

In the next moment, the incredulous guard was staring at the dart Arohn had shot into his knee. He attempted an escape by climbing over the cart where JoDan whacked him with his dustpan. The guard collapsed face down over the cart.

From his vantage point, inside the cart, Arohn shot the remaining guard in the neck where the effects of the tranquilizer were immediate, and the guard rolled onto the floor.

"Good job JoDan," praised Arohn, climbing out of the cart. "What did you hit him with?"

JoDan held up the dustpan. He was surprised that Arohn had just put the guards to sleep and not killed them. "I thought—"

"No!" Arohn chuckled. "But they are going to wish they were dead when they wake up. They'll be too sick to move for a few days."

Pulling the guard into the office, Arohn found but a single key on the guard's belt and placed it on his own. *It has to be a master.*

Reloading his dart pistol, Arohn smiled at JoDan. "We'll have to get you a holster for that dustpan. Here, do you think you can handle one of these?"

He handed JoDan his backup dart pistol which JoDan hid under the dustpan.

Arohn removed a radio control device from his vest pocket and plugged it into the back of the surveillance computer. Straddling the sleeping guard, he altered the programing of the camera systems. Then he picked up the security office phone and called Maritou.

"Sanitation," Rayloh answered.

"We've got the camera system reprogramed and are ready to proceed."

"No sign of Jamah," Rayloh told him. "We'll have to go ahead without him."

"See you at the other end. Radios for emergency only."

Arohn made a quick call to Rena. No time for pleasantries. She was ready to go.

"I can't wait to see you, Rena! Be careful!"

"You, too!"

Arohn climbed back in the cart. Part way along, they passed two guards heading for the break room. One of them recognized JoDan.

"What? What did you do, get demoted?"

"Yes, my shift-leader seems to have it in for me."

The guard said something to his companion and they laughed and kept going.

"Can I put a dart in his ass?" JoDan whispered.

"Just keep pushing."

Arohn felt the vibration of his radio.

"Something must be wrong," he muttered. "Arohn here."

"We've run into a snag," Maritou told him. "There's a squad of guards congregated in the corridor and we can't cross. We're taking the alternate route. We are leaving, now, and we'll contact you at six eighty-five."

"This may actually give us more of a strategic advantage," Arohn told her. "See you, there."

JoDan stopped the cart. They had reached the access to the service facilities that would connect them to the Abaru baths. Arohn reached out of the cart and used the master key to open the door. Inside, they passed the laundry room where several workers were engrossed in a table game. Crossing unnoticed to the elevator, they rode it to the upper-level corridor leading to the baths.

The elevator door opened. "Go right, here, and push the cart to the first door in the baths. That's the supply closet. Open the door and position the cart so I can crawl in. The guards will be watching you. So, pretend to be cleaning for a while before you go back to your quarters. This is where we will part company."

"But I want to go with you. You may need me."

"But the guards will get suspicious when the cart is still here and they can't see you cleaning."

"I can pretend that I only came to check the supplies and then push the cart back in the elevator. You turn off the live feed and I'll come back and join you."

"I'll think about it."

"Please! We're wasting time, Sir."

"Okay, okay! But only if you bring your duster—dustpan, or whatever it is."

JoDan stopped the cart next to the closet and opened the door, blocking the security camera view of Arohn crawling out with his equipment. Arohn started breaching the wall inside the closet while JoDan transferred supplies from the cart to the closet and emptied the trash bins in the baths. Then he pushed the cart back into the elevator.

By the time JoDan joined him in the closet, Arohn had made a big enough hole for them to get into the passageway.

"Okay," Arohn said, checking the time, "we're early. Stay close."

The stairs led down to the hallway leading to the prep room.

"According to the blueprints, there should be a maintenance room on our right," Arohn whispered. "This must be it."

As they entered the maintenance room, two women emerged from the prep room and walked toward them. Their hands were stained by various colors of dye. They had been prepping Anya for her execution ceremony.

JoDan had seen the older one before, and had had fantasies of her yielding to his caresses. He'd even made plans to approach her one day. But right now, she either did not notice, or did not remember him. He left the door slightly ajar and could hear their voices as they passed.

"She is so beautiful!" the younger one was saying. "It's a shame she has to die!"

"They never let us watch." the older one said, disappointed. "This is one I would really love to see."

"My sister says they will behead her. I couldn't watch that!"

"Yes, and I heard they are going to give the trophy to her lover," the older one piped in gleefully.

A chill went up JoDan's spine. His attraction to this shallow and callous woman evaporated and condensed into a shield of ice over his heart.

Arohn checked his watch. Six eighty-two. Almost time.

Had he looked into the hallway at that moment, he would have seen a hooded Gentar unlock the door to the prep room and go in.

The hallway curved to match the shape of the ship's nose. Some thirty paces to the right of the prep room, was the formal entrance to the Ceremonial Chamber with its ornate double door. Beyond that, Maritou and the others had reached their entry point.

Maritou radioed Arohn. "We're in position, and I can see the entrance to the Ceremonial Chamber from here. But no guards."

"Odd, for sure! We only saw a couple, ourselves."

"We are ready at your command."

"Okay! At the ten count—"

Arohn looked at JoDan who was itching for a fight. "You stay here, for now."

JoDan opened his mouth to protest.

"No arguments."

A moment later, Arohn was in the hallway, pushing a trash bin ahead of him for cover. He passed the prep room and stopped when he had a clear view of the Ceremonial Room entrance. No sign of guards.

Around the curve, with Maritou in the lead, the rest of the team approached, moving stealthily toward the target.

Suddenly, Rayloh sensed something from behind and swung around, coming face to face with five fully armored guards brandishing automatic weapons. The doors to the Ceremonial Chamber opened and more guards poured out.

Totally outnumbered, Maritou placed her weapon on the floor and held up her hands. One of the officers came forward and bashed her in the side of the head with the butt of his rifle.

Unable to save them, Arohn watched helplessly as Rayloh and Sten were brought to the entrance and forced to their knees. Maritou's limp body was carried into the Chamber.

Then, O'Ruhn himself appeared at the doorway. Arohn heard

him taunting Sten. "Ah! Welcome back, my son. Come in, come in! There is about to be a ceremony, and you will be my guest of honor."

Arohn weighed the options. He crawled backwards toward the kitchen before he could be detected and made his way into the prep room.

This has to be connected to the Ceremonial Chamber. Jamah must have betrayed us!

He crossed the prep room and cracked open the door at the far end. Looking out, he realized the door was hidden from the Chamber by a partition. Luck was on his side, so far. He crawled to the edge of the partition.

From his vantage point, he had glimpses of O'Ruhn chanting at the edge of the altar. Two of his minions were dancing and twirling around him to the rhythm of the ghostly music playing softly. From where he was lying on the floor, he could not see the victim on the stone alter.

O'Ruhn raised his arms above his head. He was holding a large blade in his palms, as if offering it to some unseen deity. He wore a fanciful demon mask. Its long, curled tongue seemed to wag lecherously.

"Behold the mighty power of O'Ruhn!" proclaimed a third minion.

The blade O'Ruhn held so reverently, was yet to be stained with blood.

Maybe I'm not too late. Arohn hoped.

Off to the right, Maritou, Rayloh and Sten stood, bound and fastened to poles. Sten's face was ashen, his mouth hanging open in horror. They were elevated enough to witness the carnage about to take place. A fourth Gentar, which Arohn did not recognize, was tied up with them.

Maritou spotted Arohn and nodded. Her left eye was swollen and black.

The third minion, Zelena, came forward as the music picked up in tempo and volume. The tray, she carried, held a chalice with a large cruet, and a bowl.

Arohn stood for a better firing position. He would take out

O'Ruhn with a kill shot and dispatch the minions if they offered resistance. Otherwise, there were no guards to be seen.

He now had a clear view of Anya. She was tied down on her back with her legs slightly open. Her body and face had been dyed in vivid reds, blues and greens. She was a breathtaking example of a young Abaru, known for their beauty and plump sensual flesh.

Zelena set the tray down on a table next to O'Ruhn. She then reached behind the altar, producing a woven basket which she carried around the room, placing it under her head and moving her neck in such a way as to imitate her head rolling into the basket. She provoked Sten with a venomous sneer as she danced by. Her teeth had been sharpened to needle points. Sten strained helplessly against his restraints.

Arohn would have to take his shot with impeccable timing, for the dancing minions were blocking his view and he only got momentary glimpses of his target as they twirled by.

Realizing the significance of the basket, Anya opened her mouth in panic. "Oh! Please! Don't hurt me!"

Even the inside of Anya's mouth had been dyed crimson and blue.

Zelena placed the basket on an altar, took up the cruet, and filled the chalice. Presenting it to O'Ruhn, he poured some of the liquid into a small fire pit. The flames flared high for a moment and changed color.

He held the cup as in a toast to Anya. "With this potion, I send you off to the next realm. While you still live, I will consume your flesh and you will become part of me, immortal in my consciousness."

"Behold, the mighty power of O'Ruhn!" the minions chanted.

O'Ruhn looked back at his son. Satisfied with what he found there, he smiled and handed the cup back to Zelena, who placed it to Anya's lips. She returned the cup to O'Ruhn with a bow. He drank deeply from the potion. More potion was poured and each minion drank.

The aphrodisiac effect of the potion was irresistible. Anya became lost in an altered state of consciousness.

"Come to me Sten!" Anya beckoned, struggling to open her legs to welcome him.

A minion untied her and she rolled over on to her knees, presenting her swelling organs toward her lover. The tips of her anal and vaginal tubes had been dyed to match her mouth.

One of the minions went to the bowl and dipped out a sensitizing salve and began massaging it into Anya's organs. Anya moaned in pleasure, imagining Sten inside her.

The minion's own organs had swollen beyond comfort, and she massaged them with a fresh dip from the salve bowl.

O'Ruhn removed his mask and the spectators gasped in disgust. Centuries of artificially maintaining his immortality with Abaru flesh, and the debauchery he worshiped, had transformed him into a real monster.

Maritou peered into the malevolent eyes and could find no trace of the O'Ruhn she had once loved.

Finally, Arohn had a clear shot but the minion stepped back to offer the salve bowl to O'Ruhn. The shot caught her in the back of the head and it exploded. Her headless body seemed to fall in slow motion.

O'Ruhn was gone!

"There!" shouted Sten, his forehead nodding toward the curtain behind the altar. Zelena and the other remaining minion closed ranks in front of Arohn.

Arohn swung his weapon, knocking them to the floor, and scrambled over the top of them to get to the curtain. Zelena was still conscious and grabbed his foot. He fell headlong, knocking himself senseless on the stone edge of the altar.

The curtain parted and out came O'Ruhn, flashing his blade.

"My old foe, Arohn!" he laughed and kicked the assault rifle aside.

Arohn was coming to.

"Don't move my little alien pin cushion, I'm going to end your days, here and now!"

O'Ruhn raised his blade to strike. A strange expression filled his eyes, and he stepped forward abruptly. He fell in a heap over Arohn, who wondered why he couldn't feel O'Ruhn's blade.

The handle of a small dagger protruded from O'Ruhn's back,

pulsating from the still beating heart.

The hooded figure stood at O'Ruhn's feet, removing the face covering.

"Rena!" Rayloh shouted.

Rena took a bow, quite pleased with herself.

Arohn made it to his feet, a bit unsteady, yet. He removed the robe from the minion who had tripped him. She was too frightened to protest.

Arohn was just tall enough to get his arms above the altar. He twirled the robe over Anya's nude body.

Still under the effects of the potion, Anya became lost in the sensual feel of the silky robe. She softly murmured as she moved her lips and nose across the fabric. She would awaken later, with Sten caressing her face, remembering very little of her ordeal.

Rena and Arohn released the captives. The Gentar that Arohn did not recognize was introduced to him.

"So, you are Jamah! You weren't the one who betrayed us, after all."

"No, I'm sure that was Henovar, my companion," said Rena.

"You always did know how to handle yourself," Rayloh said, embracing Rena.

"We have a lot of catching up to do," she told him.

"Yes, we do."

He kissed her forehead tenderly, and with great reverence for her strength and endurance.

Rena took Arohn and Maritou into her arms. "I knew you would one day find me."

Still clutching her friends, Rena turned to Jamah. "Would you try to get Colonel Duran on the phone?"

"My pleasure, Lady Rena."

Colonel Duran was second-in-command of the vessel. He and Rena had developed an unspoken bond over the centuries. They had exchanged only polite greetings and pleasantries but she could nonetheless sense his compassion and kinship.

Jamah came back, handing the receiver to Rena.

"Colonel Duran? This is Rena."

"Where have you been? We have been looking for you."

"Colonel Duran, take full command of the ship. O'Ruhn is dead! And arrest BarOak!"

"Are you okay?"

"Yes, everyone is fine."

"Stay where you are. I'll be right there."

Chapter 29

Identity Crisis

Back in her chambers, Rena took respite in a long shower. Rayloh would be waiting to see her after they both rested. She did not allow herself to foretell what would take place between them. She simply let the many thoughts and feelings she was having, flow by without attachment or control.

Rayloh was not "her" Gar. She knew that. Nonetheless, he was identical in most respects, but lacking the memories and experiences of the last fifteen centuries. One thing that he will have memory of, will be the time he impregnated her. His seed was still viable inside her, after so many centuries. As she imagined combining it with an egg and sending it to her uterus, she felt indescribable love for Gar.

Her life with Gar had been short. Together, they had faced a whirlwind of changes, and the time was never right to bring their child into existence. And then, she was taken from him! And now, he was light-years away, with the distance ever expanding.

"*We shall see*," she told herself. "*Whatever happens from this day forward, one thing I know—something inside me is driving me forward—I'm free now to express, to create, to live!*"

After her shower, she slept for a while before calling Rayloh. She dreamt that she was flying high above the bubble plant islands of Hogar with Gar's child. Gar joined them and the three of them morphed into a vibrating ball of light and plasma, shining its protective rays over Hogar.

Rayloh arrived and they dined together, alone. They did not engage in small talk and remained mostly silent, at first, each waiting for the right moment and the words to express their apprehensions. Toward the end of their meal, Rena proposed a toast.

"Here is to you! What shall I call you? Rayloh? Gar?"

Before he could answer, she addressed the tension she could sense.

"I know you are feeling uneasy. We both are, really!"

He nodded.

"When I found out you were here and Maritou told me who you are and that you held Gar's memories—well, there is a lot to sort out!"

"I don't quite know what to do," he admitted. "I'm experiencing something strange now that Gar's memories are combined with Rayloh's."

Her eyes encouraged him to continue.

"There aren't two of us, in here," he tried to explain, as his hands touched his head and then his breast. "We—Gar and Rayloh, are realizing that we are one. We have the same soul. There is an overriding consciousness that is guiding us through the confusion. Right now, we—no, I—I'm going through an identity crisis. What will be my role, now, in my most important relationships, including you and me? My god! How I love you and want you!"

Her muscles locked in an inner battle. She wanted to take him in her arms and surrender to the uncontrollable passion that she felt. But, as sweet as their lovemaking would surely be, it would bring consequences that would just add to their dilemma.

"Can I suggest something?" she offered.

"Of course!"

"Believe me, I want you, too! But why don't we agree to take the tension off, at least for now, and not put any expectations on each other. You have your relationship to work out, with the new and improved Naomi. And, when we all get back to Arohn's base, I will be talking with 'my Gar' who is far beyond my reach. We both have a lot ahead of us, you and I."

"I'll try," he said. "I feel that my biggest concern is for you. I don't want you to be alone, my love."

Her hands grasped his.

"I don't feel alone, and I don't intend to remain alone. And, no matter what happens, you cannot take responsibility for me. Anyway, I have a lot of plans and the strength to carry them forward. I'm going to be very busy with all the things I've been working out in my mind—during my vacation, here."

"Okay!" he said. "And to answer your first question, please call me Rayloh.

He held up his drink. "And here's to you, Lady Rena!"

When luck runs high, you may sing praises to me
I am but the canvas
Every brush stroke is applied by the momentum and
choices far away from my control
I move with the mercy of the current and I am the flood

Chapter 30

Second Chances

Maritou and her team of raiders cleared each floor as they made their way up the levels of MC3. They paused on Level Seven where she and Mantahn had entered the asteroid.

"Lieutenant Simi?" she called. "You can come out, now."

The lieutenant and his bot keeper came from behind a drilling rig from where they had been standing guard.

"Any activity to report?" Maritou asked.

"We heard some voices from above a few times and what sounded like a metal door closing. But that's it."

"Okay, you and I will go up and scout the next level before the others advance."

The eighth and nineth levels were scouted and cleared. Maritou and Simi were scouting the tenth level when a door opened. They came face to face with two startled Vulans coming out to see why they had lost contact with their comrades.

"Freeze!" Maritou ordered.

The pair were unarmed. One complied timidly and the other looked put out but said nothing.

Maritou left Simi to cover them and proceeded into the interior of a large laboratory. It was packed with incubators, each with a Vulan occupant in various stages of development; each one identical to the next. On shelves, to one side, was a supply of helmets. They were like the ones adorned by the fallen defenders she had seen on the second level. Three more workers were in the nursery attending to their harvest. They surrendered to Maritou without a struggle.

Next to the helmets, a fully developed Vulan lay strapped to an operating table. Several wires extended from probes implanted through the skull.

"Who's in charge here?" Maritou insisted.

Nobody spoke, but all eyes pointed to the puffed-up one standing in the doorway.

"I am A'Vanoff, Doctor Ilee A'Vanoff."

"Well, A'Vanoff, do you know what you are doing?"

"Of course, I do!"

"Listen, Ilee-A! There's nobody left down below to come to your aid. We're going upstairs. What are we going to find up there?"

The mad doctor folded his arms and gave Maritou a defiant sneer.

"Ok! Play it that way. But if we run into any unpleasant surprises, I'm going to come down here myself and, well—" she said calmly, patting the handle of her knife for effect. "You don't want to see me coming."

He couldn't decide if she was bluffing or not, but he wisely decided not to chance it.

"Okay, okay! The next floor up is another nursery that is being prepared for more production. The incubators are still empty. Next, are the living quarters and dining hall for most of the crew. Above that, I'm not sure. Nobody is allowed to go there, but I do think that there is a command center up there. But I don't know what else.

"Who do you answer to?"

Again, he hesitated.

"It's Ben Ru, isn't it?"

"Well—yes. I get all my orders directly from him. I haven't seen him for a while now.

"Ok."

She pointed to the motionless being on the operating table.

"Will they die if you don't attach the helmets?"

"What does it matter? They have no memories," he scoffed, regaining some of his starch.

"I didn't ask for your asinine opinion! What can be done to keep them alive without installing the helmets?"

"Obviously you know nothing about replication." he ridiculed. "They would eventually need memory installation but can live for a while if left in the incubators."

"And that's what you and your flunkies here are going to do. You'll stay here and care for them. You're under house arrest until our people can get here to take over."

"You can't arrest me!"

Maritou called for three of her Vulan soldiers led by a crusty sergeant.

"Sergeant, detain these—gentlemen. They are going to stay here and take care of their—their patients. Shoot any of them that get out of line but, whatever you do, don't arrest them."

"Yes ma'am!"

The next two levels were much like A'Vanoff had described, and the raiders did not run into any resistance. The crew that had been setting up the new nursery were found hiding in a supply closet.

The cooks and cleaning crew on the residential level were taken completely by surprise. They did not hear the battle that had taken place, below, because the main elevator shaft did not extend to the levels above the nurseries. The upper levels had their own elevator system.

There were only two ways to access the upper levels from where they were now, the stairway or the one elevator from the residential level. Maritou called for the demolition crew to assess the best access route. A short time, later, the crew leader reported that the stairway access was blocked by a thick door that would require heavy blasting. The elevator car was stopped at a level beyond the next level up, so the elevator door on the next level could be accessed and cracked open. It was unknown what was on the other side. She gave the order to go through the elevator shaft.

In the meantime, she gathered her Gentars. With Lieutenant Simi and Corporal le Gauhn, his bot handler, there were six including Maritou.

"Mantahn, you and Corporal le Gauhn will stay here unless I call for you. The rest of us will enter the upper level. Simi, you will come right behind me, then Sergeant Akini, Private Hatah and Private Jenah. If we are killed, you're in charge, Mantahn. If all else fails, you can stand guard and wait for reinforcements. Arohn will come when he has completed the raid on Solay Mahn."

The demolition crew leader appeared.

"We have the door open, Ma'am."

"What did you find on the other side?"

"It just leads to a small compartment, only large enough for one person at a time. There's a door on the inside that seems to be unlocked. Do you want us to open it?"

"No, I'll open it. It could be a trap."

She thanked the demolition crew and turned to her Gentars.

"Here we go!"

The entry room was indeed small, just large enough for Maritou to get down on her knees to make herself a smaller target once the door was opened. She put her hand on the cool metal and started to push, slowly—

"Get out!" Simi screamed to the others coming behind him.

Maritou looked and her Lieutenant turned head down and disappeared in an instant. She felt a rush of stale air coming from the elevator shaft as she was about to stick her head inside to find out what happened to the rest of her team. Something—some instinct stopped her, and the elevator cabin whizzed by, crashing into the bottom of the shaft.

She grabbed her radio. "Simi?" she implored.

A sickening silence settled on her shoulders like a heavy black cloak. Time held her in paralysis.

"Yes! Maritou! Are you okay?"

The sudden incident had placed her in an illusory state. The fingertips of her left hand clasped the bridge of her nose, slowing the discharge of her emotions, holding back tears that she didn't understand.

"Yes—I'm in one piece. How are you, and the others?"

"We made it out, just in time. We'll come back and join you, but it will take a bit of time. The shaft is completely blocked."

"I'm going in!" she asserted. "Whoever tried to crush us wants to slow us down. Get to me when you can. I don't have time to talk any longer."

Pushing the door open, slowly, she looked down a long and empty hallway. Progressing to the first door in a crouching stance, she paused at the threshold. Her partial view of the interior indicated that this must me the command center.

Silence.

Still carrying the camera probe, she had used to penetrate the emergency hatch, she peeked inside the command room.

Bodies?

She entered the command room to find the bodies of two Gentars sitting side by side. Their weapons were holstered. Their heads had been violently smashed together.

No sign of struggle. They must have known and trusted their assassin.

She went back and continued to the end of the hallway, which turned in two directions. The turn to the right led to the stairway and the other to another hallway with several doors on its right side. The rooms behind the doors proved to be sleeping quarters which she cleared, one at a time—all empty.

Now to the stairwell where she would be vulnerable. Again, she used the camera probe. Someone was standing in the doorway on the left side of the landing, above. She watched him peek around the corner occasionally.

It's a Vulan.

He apparently had not spotted the small end of the probe. She noticed that the tip of his machine gun barrel was visible each time his head appeared. By the position of the barrel, she knew that he carried his machine gun in his left hand.

He must be right-handed. This means that, to use it, he'll need to bring it up and around his body, in order to get his finger on the trigger. That will slow him down. I'll have the advantage of surprise, speed and probably accuracy.

Having more faith in her bow, she set her machine pistol on the floor. She waited until his head retracted once more, and timed her movements. Silently she sprang up the stairs on foot and took flight, just as the face reappeared. Her arrow impacted the machine gun. He dropped it and ran.

Maritou had no time to recover her own machine pistol. She grabbed his weapon and pursued him into a labyrinth of hallways and chambers. Whichever way he went, she couldn't determine.

Methodically clearing rooms as she went, she heard something inside what looked to be a prison cell door. She threw open the latch and stepped back.

"Come out of there! Whoever is in there, step out here now!"

Pop!

The small explosion came from behind her. And with it, a sharp pain at the base of her neck. She reached back and pulled out the projectile as she spun to face her attacker. She had been darted and the anesthetic was taking immediate effect.

As she dropped to her knees, she recognized her attacker. She had never seen him face to face, but only in photographs.

He was upon her and pulled her head back to cut her throat. Unable lift her arms to defend herself, she waited for the coup de grace.

And then she must have gone unconscious because she was surely dreaming. She dreamt that a Gentar stepped from the prison cell. She knew him, too, but not from any photograph! Then the two men were locked in a wrestling match for the knife. In her dream, she was lying in bed and stared in horror as the Gentar twisted the Vulan's head around so far, she thought it would pop off.

She awoke with soft hands gently stroking her face.

"Mihn? Is that you?" she wondered.

"No, my precious Maritou, it's me!"

"O'Ruhn! O'Ruhn! How can this be?"

"You saved me, Maritou! Your love saved me! We've been here on the Armada the whole time."

"We?"

He motioned to the dead Vulan.

BarOak!

"What?"

"Our DNA and memory crystals were smuggled in by Ben Ru. And, we stayed dormant until Dr. A'Vanoff learned the secrets of replication."

O'Ruhn winced and grabbed his side. Blood was pooling on the floor beside him.

"You're hurt!"

"Yes, and there are a few things I want to say while I'm still conscious," he said.

She tried to get up so she could tend to his wounds. Even though she had pulled out the dart before it injected its full payload, she wouldn't be able to stand for a while. All she could do was listen.

"My biggest regret is my treatment of Rena. When I became aware again, here on this asteroid, I was told that I kidnapped her as the Armada was leaving. Do you know where I took her? Does she still live?"

"Yes, she does! And I may be talking to her, soon. You want me to ask for her forgiveness?"

"Not for my sake, but for hers."

Another wave of pain crashed over O'Ruhn and he murmured his lament. "You see, until you came to me in an apparition and spoke to me, the resentment I felt was unbearable. It fed more resentment and pain. I don't want that for her, or for Gar. I love them both and I have done them so much harm! But you helped me! Just knowing you was a lesson in right action. And then you came to me in spirit and told me that it was not too, late! That's when I decided I needed a second chance and I let BarOak record my memories. Ben Ru smuggled our DNA codes and memory crystals aboard the Armada. It just hasn't turned out the way I had it pictured."

"I will let Rena and Gar know. Were you also told that you have a son?"

O'Ruhn reeled at this. "Why no, I wasn't!"

"His name is Sten. And things haven't worked out well with that relationship either. He could use some words from you, too. He has only known the monster that you slowly became. I've never talked to him but the other Maritou knows him well. She's been like a mother for him. She tells me he is turning out to be a fine young Gentar."

"I can imagine the harshness he must face. Tell him I am very proud of him and would do anything, if only I could."

Another grimace cast its shadow over O'Ruhn's handsome face and tears formed. Having difficulty kneeling, he lay down next to her.

"Why were you locked up in that cell?" she wondered.

"When I learned the asteroid was being invaded, I wanted to help. I went to the Command Room and killed the two officers. I tried to kill BarOak, too, but he got the drop on me and locked me in that cell. You need to know that there is someone else locked up, here."

"Mihn Rova!"

O'Ruhn 's voice was fading. "Yes, do you know her?"

"I know her replica."

Maritou sensed that O'Ruhn was close to death.

"Take care of her, Maritou. Take care of Mihn. She's endured a lot."

"Where is your genetic code, O'Ruhn?"

"Don't have me replicated. I've achieved what I came here to do. I pity my original. He will surely face a bitter end! Thank you, Maritou—I love you!"

She looked into his eyes. "I love you, too!"

"I'm going to sleep, now," he said softly, and closed his eyes.

Chapter 31

Sisterhood

Maritou came home late and exhausted from her combat mission. She wanted to tell Gar everything. But, now, she just wanted to sleep. Food and conversation would wait until morning.

Gar wanted all the details, of course, but knew she just wanted him to lie next to her with his arm around her waist as she fell asleep. So overjoyed to have her back and in one piece, the smell of the salve on her wings didn't stop him from burying his face in her back.

When morning came, Gar had a big breakfast made for them, and she ate her share and half of his. Only then, did she start filling him in on the highlights of her ordeal.

He remained quiet when she told the tale of O'Ruhn and BarOak. At first, she didn't know how he was reacting to O'Ruhn's words of regret. She just told it as it happened, and did nothing to influence his thoughts and emotions.

When she had finished, his face was solemn and his eyes were moist with tears that did not fall. She had seen this before, and knew this happened at the peak of his emotions. But this time, he sat with it and didn't retreat by stuffing things that were difficult to accept.

Finally, he spoke, and with emotion. "He was my best friend, O'Ruhn was. Like a brother, I loved him. The greatest hurt I've ever suffered, aside from the loss of Rena, was his betrayal. My dilemma is that forgiveness is an elusive goal and, even if I can find some of it for the version of O'Ruhn that came here, there will always be the other O'Ruhn. And, at the heart of it, my soul's cry for justice is fueling my anger. Right now, I am unsure whether forgiveness is even the right thing to do, or not. Forgiveness can never be denial, or trying to forget, or making excuses for the offender. Those things are not forgiveness, and I've found them to be harmful.

"And I know this," he continued. "I have a right to my anger. And that gives me the right to give it up. It's the crux of my dilemma. Even though I know it would make me feel better, it seems like it would be a gift to the person that wronged me. Can you forgive him, Maritou?"

"Not on your behalf. He wronged me by hurting the people that I love. And that is the only thing that I have the right to forgive."

"How do you do it? I mean, what is the process? What can I be doing differently?"

"I can only speak for myself. In O'Ruhn's case, the one back on Hogar, he is not repentant and that makes it more difficult for me because I don't believe he is worthy of forgiveness. But what I find, is that I am still able to find some compassion, at least. And that allows me to start clearing a path to forgiving. For me, it is a process and I have to work at it."

"Thank you, my darling. That gives me something to think about, and some hope."

After this, Gar needed to release some tension.

"I'm going to the gym. Do you want to come?" he asked.

"No. I just want to stay here and rest this morning—maybe do some stretching.

"What if I give you one of my special massages before I go? "

"Oh yes! Give me time to bathe. Would you come in and help me scrub my wings?"

"And other things."

"You may not make it to the gym!"

It was lunchtime when Gar returned home from exercise. Maritou greeted him at the door. She was excited about something.

"Arohn called while you were out. Rena has been liberated! Everyone survived the rescue operation."

Gar stood there, speechless for a moment as Maritou took him in her arms.

"It's wonderful," she whispered, and allowed him time to experience the moment in his own way.

"Let's go straight to the Command Center." he suggested.

De Vul was waiting for them when they arrived.

"Splendid news!" he greeted them. "We've received more information from Hogar."

"When can we talk to her?" Gar asked, impatiently.

"It won't be long," de Vul assured his compadre, firmly squeezing his shoulder. "They are resting and waiting for reinforcements. From where they are now, we can't patch them through to the Quantum Radio. But soon, they will take Rena back with them to Field Command."

Maritou managed to maintain her composure as she witnessed Gar agonize restlessly. She was taking everything in, moment to moment, thankful for the benevolent but mixed feelings she was having towards the reunion that was about to take place over the vast and widening expanse.

"Fifteen hundred years of captivity!" Gar exclaimed.

"My dear and wonderful friend!" Maritou trumpeted as Gar took her in his arms.

"O'Ruhn is dead," de Vul told them. "Rena killed him herself. It turns out that she rescued her rescuers."

"That doesn't surprise me at all." Maritou laughed. "Fifteen hundred years, indeed! But it didn't take away her fierce spirit."

"There were some tense moments," de Vul explained, "but the only casualties on our side were a few bumps and bruises. Things didn't go so well for O'Ruhn, though. He was just about to cut le Noir's throat when a small blade was expertly placed between his ribs. It was Rena, of course! She had maneuvered her way into O'Ruhn's Ceremonial Chamber through a labyrinth of passageways and air ducts that she had explored over the centuries. Otherwise, the entire rescue team would surely be dead."

"Good for her!" Lore Li piped in.

"The bad news is that BarOak managed to escape," de Vul informed them. "But he is not an immediate threat. President Dahl has already had General Dulah arrested and they are rounding up all of O'Ruhn's known allies. The only significant military opposition facing le Noir, now, are the forces that were attacking Vul. And the enemy fleet cannot hold out very long without support from Hogar. BarOak will most likely reach the Vulan stronghold on Eo Phi's moon where he can elude le Noir indefinitely."

"I'm going to wait here, by the radio, until we hear directly from Rena," Gar declared.

Sensing that her presence was adding to the tension, Maritou took her leave. "I'll stay close by if you need me."

Gar kissed her. "I love you!" he told her. "Thank you!"

"I love you, too!" And she walked to her office to wait.

Arohn and Lore Li withdrew to his office. Arohn had something to tell her. "There is something I haven't told anyone yet. But I want to tell you, now, Lore Li."

Lore Li had come to feel Arohn's high regard for her. Her love and passion for him had magnified, as had the heart sickness from being so close to a thing one cherishes but cannot have; the thing that one can see but not touch.

"Cole came to see me," Arohn began.

"Yes?"

"When his agents went to make arrests at the Centex Group, they searched everything." Arohn's face turned solemn. "They found my wife's DNA records and memory crystals."

Lore Li's reaction surprised her. The tears that erupted did not contain the bitter essence of her own loss—that would come later—they flowed sweet and clear with the love that filled her heart. Her arms went around him and she kissed his cheek.

"Oh Arohn! I am so happy for you!" *Now he can restore his lost love. Lan Loa will come back to him.*

"But you don't understand! It's that I can no longer run from the truth. You see, this has released me."

"What do you mean?" She began to step back but he was holding her in place.

"The truth is that I no longer love her the way I did. Restoring her to me, the way I am now, would be to live a lie. She deserves better, and so do I."

Lore Li could only look at him with astonishment.

"Someday," he went on, "there will be a place and time for them. Lan Loa and another Arohn can be restored, together, with the memory crystals that were recorded back before her murder, back when their love was boundless. That is what they deserve."

Lore Li's heart picked up a cadence of expectation.

"You see, I've fallen in love with someone else," he told her. "Will you have me?"

"You would have to be a fool not to know that!" she gushed.

She gripped him behind the neck and pulled his lips to hers. Their kiss became a fountain, flowing into a river of passion.

"I want this to last forever!" he told her.

In her office, Maritou waited. To occupy some time, she cleaned out her desk and carried the blueprints for O'Ruhn's vessel, to the filing room.

The clerk smiled knowingly. "Waiting is the hardest part, isn't it?"

"Sometimes, that's the case," Maritou conceded.

She returned to her empty office and sat. To avoid churning out wild thoughts, she tried to think again of the experiments she and Gar had been working on before life had taken so many detours.

She was interrupted by a maintenance worker carrying a cot.

"This was ordered by the gal in the file room. Where shall I set it?"

"How thoughtful! Just put it right there, please."

After that, she tried go back to her plans for the next experiment, but soon succumbed to the beckoning of the empty cot. Still recovering from the stresses of the previous day, she closed her eyes and was soon asleep.

She dreamt she was back on Hogar, soaring effortlessly over small uninhabited floating islands, whisked along in streams of cool air. It was a return to the day she and Rena had met Gar and O'Ruhn. There were two figures standing on an approaching island, waving to her. As she drew closer, she realized they were Gar and Rena. And then she heard them calling her name. Struggling to join them, she could not break free of the current. As she was pulled, farther and farther away from them, their cries turned into an annoying ringing sound.

She awoke, drenched in sweat. It took her a moment to distinguish her ringing portable from the surreal buzzing in her dream.

It was the Communications Center. Rena had made it to Field Command and was talking with Gar.

Maritou had anticipated this moment and had imagined her reaction to be much different from the way she now felt. She could not seem to shake the horrible feeling from her dream. She was exhausted and wanted to return to the cot.

Instead, she went to freshen up and then to the Communication Center.

Taking a seat in the inner reception area, she could see Gar, behind a glass partition, talking to Rena.

"This could take a while," she told herself.

What am I going to say to her? Hello Rena—Long time no see. And, by the way, I'm in love with your husband?

Will this be the end of our friendship? The end of Gar and me?

Her uncertainty grew. Time crept by.

Finally, Gar emerged. He had a look of peace that she had never witnessed.

"She's waiting to talk to you," he said, holding the door for her, smiling.

Was there a message in his smile? She couldn't tell. She simply nodded and went in, settling uneasily in front of the Quantum Radio.

"Rena?"

"Yes, my love! I'm here."

"I— I just can't believe it. You're alive!"

"Yes, I am. I won't try to tell you what it has been like for me over the past centuries. All I'll say is that I never lost hope, and it has been the love of Gar, and you, that has kept me going."

"Oh, Rena! I love you! And for so long, I felt that my love for Gar was a betrayal."

"I know you, Maritou, and I know you feel that way without you telling me. But let me tell you—you and Gar?—that is exactly what I have hoped for both of you!"

"Really?"

"Yes! I remember the moment you and I met him."

Maritou laughed. "Yes, he was trying to impress us with his flying skills and he crashed into a Flowering Semor! He was ogling us instead of watching where he was going."

"That's right," Rena chuckled. "And I fell in love with him on the spot. I never told you, but I knew you did, too."

"Yes, I did!"

"So, what could have been better for the two people I love the most? I can only imagine what you must be feeling now, with me back in the picture. You are wondering how this will change the life you have come to know with Gar, aren't you?"

"Yes! I can't deny that. But, at the same time, I'm experiencing this wonderful change. For so long, I didn't believe in myself, and I think I blamed others for it to divert the responsibility away from myself."

"Gar loves you, Maritou, and he doesn't want to lose you. My reappearance doesn't change that."

"What about you, Rena? I cannot fathom the thought of you being alone!"

"I've had a long time to grieve my losses. Just because I am alone, now, doesn't mean I will be forever. Anyway, I am excited about the work I want to do here. And that is going to keep me occupied for a long time to come."

"Please tell me more!"

"Well, Rayloh can now return to Operation Freedom and remove the collision threat from Vespi, putting it in a higher, safe orbit. But, as I'm sure you know, we also have the longer-term problem of runaway greenhouse gases, here on Hogar. We need a radical solution and I have given this much thought during my captivity."

"What do you have in mind?"

"Well, there are many feasible alternatives. We have all of the resources here in the solar system to create livable environments for ourselves on other planets if we cannot save Hogar. But perhaps our biggest challenge will be to get the people of Hogar on board with some type of plan. Right now, they aren't even aware of the environmental problem with global warming. O'Ruhn made sure of that."

"I'm so happy you are alive and safe. I envy Venahus being able to be there with you in the flesh. But I have you now, too, in my thoughts and over the Quantum Two-Way. And I believe that one day, one of us will cross the great expanse that separates us."

"We'll see."

Epilogue

What are your plans now that your work here is completed?" Cole wondered.

"My first priority is to relax," Maritou told him.

"That's not going to last long if I know you."

"I'm just feeling so good, today, Cole, I'm ready to set all of life's struggles aside for a while. I came here, to your office, directly from a meeting with the Renewal Board."

She laughed. "I think I frighten them. But I don't care. They are going to recommission Vinnie! Gar and I have agreed that we want to take care of him while he transitions into his new life."

"Oh, Maritou, I'm so happy!"

"And how are things with Mihn?" She probed.

Cole and Mihn had just returned from a two-day getaway to explore their plans for the future.

"We're in love! And, I've been such an idiot for so long. We are going to take it kind of slow, right now, because Mihn will be busy nursing her Original back from the deprivations she's suffered."

"I haven't met her, yet," Maritou mentioned. "I was out cold when you and Arohn came and released her from the lab."

"She talks a lot about O'Ruhn. In the short time he was there, it seems he was very soft-hearted with her, and it helped her regain hope and a positive attitude. She's devastated over his death."

"I'm convinced that he was genuinely repentant," Maritou said. "I'm struggling though with the way he chose to escape from the person he was becoming. Do you think he took the coward's way out?"

"You mean by sending himself into the future and not really making any meaningful changes at the time?"

"Exactly!" Maritou exclaimed.

"Yes, I believe he took the easy way out, without regard to the consequences to the millions of innocents back on the Planets."

"Do you know? Were his DNA and memory crystals recovered?"

"Yes, Arohn has them and hasn't decided what to do with them, yet," Cole told her. "By the way, he was here to see me earlier, this morning. He had just come from a Special Session of Council. They have abandoned the choice of a radical trajectory, but the majority remain committed to colonize W-292, even if it is proven that the two habitable planets are already vibrant with intelligent life. But they have to change the Constitution to do that. So, things are up in the air."

"I haven't had a chance to talk to Arohn, yet, about how things played out on the Solay Mahn raid. Have you arrested Dulamar?" Maritou asked.

"We don't have any hard evidence to pin on him. We thought we would find that he was producing the attack bots. But as we now know, the insects were farmed in Mihn's lab and we found no physical evidence to prove that Dulamar manufactured the helmets for the insects or for the Vulan soldiers. He certainly has the technology, but we think he disposed of the evidence after the attack on Vinnie."

"That's disappointing," said Maritou.

"Yes, and he seems to have more power than ever. He is the one leading the effort make changes to the Constitution."

"Looks like we are in for a wild ride!" Maritou said ruefully.

Acknowedgments

Creating and completing this, my first book, has been both a challenging and very exciting process. *Power of the Dark Realm* would not have achieved its success without the help and encouragement of others. Somehow, I was fortunate to be guided to the right people.

Once that I felt satisfied with, what I considered to be my final manuscript, I discovered that there was a lot more to do before the first copy hit the shelves. There are two people who really took the reins when this time came. One was my publisher, of course, who I will thank separately. The other is my friend Jim Arthurs who has stepped up and filled so many gaps and has provided practically everything needed to promote my novel.

Jim is an animator and filmmaker by trade. Over the last 38 years he has provided visual effects for commercials and films. Using artificial intelligence and his own artwork, he created the layout and artwork for the book cover and the animations and artwork for the social media and website "Book Trailers". You are amazing, Jim! Thank you!

My publisher, Donald Kallaus, and I met a little over a year ago. From the beginning, Don took a genuine interest in my book and has encouraged me in ways that he may not even be aware. In our first meeting, after he read the preliminary manuscript, he remarked, "I wouldn't be embarrassed to publish your book." We chuckled over his light-hearted compliment but it stuck with me. And Don stuck with me throughout the long process of creating the final manuscript. I guess that comes with the years of experience he has in the publishing business. Thank you, Don!

As my final draft was coming into focus, I decided to seek the feedback and guidance of an expert writer and teacher. Since I had known another student of Jim Ciletti's, I naturally went to see him. Jim took a large section of my work and spent hours with me, teaching me how to improve my writing style. Jim told me something during the time we spent together. He said he wanted me to think of myself as a story teller. I think of that comment often. Somehow it is helping me to find my voice. Thank you, Jim! Jim is the co-owner and operator of Hooked on Books, in Colorado Springs.

When I told my friend and fellow writer, Dr. Fran Pilch that I was writing a novel, she offered to proof read it for me. I wonder if she would have done that, had she known what she had in store. She spent many hours extracting the excess commas that I had used so generously. She dubbed me "The Comma King"! Oh! By the way, Fran, the next book is on the way! But seriously, thank you for the wonderful help! I know my readers will thank you, too.

Appendix – Characters, Places and Things

Principle Characters

Maritou Venahus and Maritou le Rohn – Gentar Original and Copy – sometimes known to each other as "Venahus" and "Number II" 1, 7, 9, 31

Gar Lahn – Gentar Co-Commander of Armada and Scientist

Arohn de Vul (Armada Co-Commander) Vulan Original and Arohn le Noir "The Protector" (de Vul's Copy and Commander of the resistance in the home solar system) – Known to each other as "de Vul" and "le Noir" 5, 6, 9

Rena – Gar's wife – held captive by O'Ruhn 3, 9, 53

O'Ruhn – Gentar underground ruler on Hogar – former friend of Gar 3, 24, 35, 94, 101, 159

Lore Li de Mohn – de Vul's Vulan aide in the Command Center 23, 179

Rayloh Cari – Gar's clone 31, 42, 148

Naomi Kamara – Rena's clone 31, 42

Col. BeCholn – Gentar Security Chief for the Armada – Nick name "Cole" 37, 74

Mihn Rova – Gentar entomologist and developer of bio-robotic technologies 70, 74, 184

Vin Pah Dumah – "Newborn" Gentar – Former student and close friend of Maritou 83, 84, 105, 184

Sten – O'Ruhn's son 7, 32, 55, 65, 72, 148

BarOak – O'Ruhn's Vulan lieutenant – former lab chief during the Vulan invasion of Hogar 14, 24, 35, 102, 164, 179

Other Characters

Mendon Dahl – Maritou's former combat instructor and once lover – political foe of O'Ruhn and current President of Hogar. 8, 179

Dar Enock – Vulan botanist, former wife of Brim Lou (member of O'Ruhn's inner circle) 25, 30, 34

Capt. Ben Ru former name Sy Morah – spy and ally of O'Ruhn – Code Name "Bakus" 36, 38, 49, 51, 70, 95, 118, 135

Sauhn Lin – Ben Ru's body guard 45, 49, 55, 83, 84, 93, 120, 136

Cli Oberdahn – friend of Mihn's and member of the Armada Council 79

Mi Dulamar – Vulan Senior Councilman – (The Council is the law-making arm of the Armada government) 79, 91, 134, 185

Sumahl Dulamar – Mi Dulamar's brother and manufacturing engineer on the Solay Mahn Array

Nahmed Hosah – Gentar tycoon 92

Adil de NakshahOak – Vulan recluse – Warehouseman on the MerCon Group 97

Mylas Eberhus – Gentar sculptress and keeper of the lost art of leaf folding 92, 94

Lan Loa – de Vul's murdered wife 26, 38, 179

Mern de Kornah – Vin's Vulan math teacher 87

JoDan – dock worker on O'Ruhn's vessel 151

Jamah – Butler on the flagship/mutual friend of Rena and Sten 151, 160, 163

Anya – Sten's fiancée 101, 154, 158, 161

Col. Duran – O'Ruhn's flagship commander 163

Asteroids, Planets, Star Systems and Bubble Plant Islands

Centex Asteroid Group – Asteroid array where the main telescope observatories are located 119, 136

Mon Mari – Large bubble plant island and capitol of Hogar 13, 66, 73, 116

Solay Mahn – Manufacturing asteroid array 79, 93, 96, 141

MerCon Group – Warehouse asteroid array 129, 141

MC3 – 3rd asteroid of MerCon 97, 129, 141

Regan Group – Agricultural array 113

Asteroid B-112 – The Weightless Lab – Small asteroid with near-zero gravity 22, 40, 58

W-292 – Single white star system with two habitable planets 103, 120, 134, 185

Indersol Group – Supply and maintenance array 128

Vespi – A dwarf planet with a degrading orbit that is in a death dance with Hogar 30

Eo Phi – Hogar size planet in orbit between Hogar and Vul. In the current state of its evolution, it is uninhabited and oxygen poor. 30, 179

Other Data

The "Newborns" – Children of the Armada crewmembers born on the Mission 63, 85

"Life Blood" – Genetically modified fungus developed by Rena – Staple diet of the Vulans 36, 52

Quantum Two-Way – Radio system allowing instantaneous communications between any two points in space 3, 13, 14, 55, 154

Bunuit – Gentar delicacy   Crablike critters with a firm, mild tasting flesh – best served with Bitter Berry fruit sauce 5

Flowering Semor – Plant on Hogar 182

About the Author

Power of the Dark Realm is my first published work. If you like the characters in this novel, I have more in the pipeline. There is a lot more to the saga of the Gentars and Vulans and its characters have become an imaginary family to me. In a way they represent my belief in the inherent goodness in human kind and our potential for continued evolvement and purpose.

The best ideas usually come to me on my morning bike rides when I am away from the tax office and the phones. *A tax man?* Well, a fella has to make a living! Some might think it romantic, but I don't have the strength to be a starving artist. Anyway, there are many aspects of the workaday world that are actually fulfilling. I like to think that my real job is making my clients' lives easier.

Anyway, even during the heat of tax season, I have found time to do a little writing, here and there, even if it only amounts to recording my bike riding inspirations. *Do I feel guilty when I neglect my office duties?* All I can say is, *Thank goodness for the guy or gal that invented the extension!*

The other day, I was having a chat with a friend and he asked me if I would consider writing about some of my true-life experiences. Well, there is a story of survival, there, but I'm not ready to write it. For now, he will just have to get glimpses of me through the characters in my books: and not necessarily the heroes. Right now, I am having fun with fiction and I'll stick with that for a while.

I'm currently writing a novel focused on artificial intelligence. AI is destined to change our lives and cultures in unpredictable ways. My challenge is to point out the dangers while telling a story that is entertaining. I can't imagine me writing something that didn't include a love story or that swerved away from science fiction.

I invite you to tell me what you think. You can find contact information on my website at www.gardnermcadams.com.